BOOK ONE
DANGEROUS JOURNEY

CLARK SELBY

Library of Congress Control Number: 2024925801

ISBN
979-8-89641-009-6 (Paperback)
979-8-89641-010-2 (eBook)
979-8-89641-008-9 (Hardcover)

1

Dr. Chance Taylor and his best friend Dr. Charles Brown were spending their afternoon coffee break talking about Chance's decision to take two months off from work at Sandia National Laboratory to enter the Moscow to Beijing Road Race for classic sports cars from the nineteen-fifties.

Chance says, "Charlie you got to come with me and be my co-pilot for this race, it's going to be a wonderful experience. I'm going to ship my Corvette by ocean and travel with the car on the same ship. Come on, what do you think?"

"I'll tell you what I think, if I go home and tell Cheryl I'm taking two months off from work to go off racing a car across Russia and China, she'll tell me I'm out of my ever loving mind. That's what I think."

"Come on Charlie, you know we need to get away from all of the pressure we are under here at work, and you told me yourself you need to get some time away from Cheryl and the kids to have a chance to save your marriage."

"Yeah, get away, but not go crazy."

"Charles, I'll tell you what I'll do. I'll pay all of your expenses for the trip and throw in airline tickets for your wife and daughters to go to Chicago to visit her folks for the summer."

"Cheryl's never going to go for me being gone for two months."

"Charlie, we've haven't take more than a week off since we started college and we've already been at Sandia for almost ten years, we deserve a break, a big break. Come on, it will be good for you and who do you know that's offering you a better deal than the one I just gave you?"

"OK, Chance against my better judgment. I'll talk to Cheryl about it when I get home tonight, OK?"

"OK, good man, you'll see we'll have a great time and maybe we will win the race and I'll split the two-hundred and fifty thousand dollar prize money with you."

"Sure and I going to be promoted to the Director of Sandia, when we return after being gone for two months, I don't think so!"

"Charlie, you never can tell what happens next. Did you ever think when we started college we'd be nuclear physics working on nuclear weapon systems at GE and saving America."

"No my goals were not that lofty. I just wanted to lay as many women on campus that I could."

"Yeah, I don't think you missed many."

"Thanks for the vote of confidence. I'll talk to Cheryl tonight, OK."

"Just turn on that old Charlie's charm, you know Cheryl can't resist it."

True to his word Charles approached Cheryl about him going with Chance on the big race as they were getting ready for bed. He was surprised when she told him she thought it would do both of them good.

She was not as thrilled when he told her they would be gone for two months, but the pain eased when he told her. Chance was picking up all of his expenses, as well as hers and the girl's airline tickets to Chicago.

Charles left early for work the next morning to get over the next hurdle he had before he could tell Chance it was a go for him on the racing trip. He drove across town and stopped at a large condo complex. He approached apartment One "A" took out his key and opened the door.

Charles called out, "Kerida, are you up?"

"I'm in the bathroom taking a bath Charlie."

Charles opened the bathroom door and saw Kerida relaxing in the tub with her feet propped up on the wall of the tub. He got down on his knees in front of the tub and kissed her hard on her lips.

Kerida said, "Charlie what are you doing here so early in the morning?"

"I need to talk with you. Chance has asked me to go with him on that road race from Moscow to Beijing and I need to know if it's all right with you?"

"Just how long would you be gone, you know I die, when I don't have you at least twice a week?"

"Two months."

"Absolutely not, you can't leave me for two months it is bad enough I have to share you with Cheryl. I'll die if you're gone that long."

"Listen baby, I need to get away before I do something crazy. I've got to get away from Cheryl for awhile, she's driving me nuts."

"So why don't you divorce her, so we can be together all of the time."

"You know, we've been over it a million times."

"Yes, we've been over it and over it, but it doesn't make any sense to me, you know I love you."

"And I love you, but I just can't leave my girls. They need me."

"I need you too, if you have to go then go."

Charles leaned back down and kissed her and said, "Thank you baby, I'll see you tonight."

As soon as she got out the bathtub, she called her brother Anmend in Chicago.

When he answered the phone she begin crying and telling him Charles was going to leave her for two months and Anmend asked her where he was going?

"He going on a stupid road race with Chance Taylor, can you believe it?"

"They are going to be gone for two months on a road race, my God where on earth are they going?"

"The stupid race is from Moscow to Beijing."

"Kerida just quit crying, why don't we go with them and you two can be together for two months without Cheryl, she not going is she?"

"I don't know. I don't think so. I can ask him when he comes back tonight, Anmend would you really do this for me?"

"You know I'll do anything for you. Kerida, you find out all of the details of the trip and I'll talk to Charles and see about us accompanying them. Hey, this could be something good for all of us."

"OK Anmend, I'll call you when I have the details of the trip."

Chance was already in the lab working by the time Charles arrived and told him the news, "I'm going with you."

"Great news, just wait you'll see we're going to have a real adventure."

Charles stopped by to see Kerida on his way home from work and he told her all of the details of his trip, all about traveling with the car by ship from New Orleans to Odessa, with stops on the island of Madeira; Gibraltar and Istanbul before arriving in Odessa.

The ocean voyage will take almost a month. On the return trip they will be flying back from Beijing.

As soon as a little lovemaking was over, Charles was out the door and Kerida was on the phone to her brother.

Anmend told her not to worry he would call Charles and tell him they wanted to go along to help. He was sure he wouldn't have any objections from Charles with that idea.

Next, he would have Charles get Chance's OK for them to come on the trip and he was sure his old friend Charles could do it all right, since Chance was one of Anmend's old friends too.

Anmend found it was easy to get Charles to agree for him and Kerida to go on the trip with them.

Chance agreed, since he knew Anmend was always a lot of fun to be with and Kerida was fluent in several languages, including Russian and Mandarin Chinese, which could be a big help to them on the trip. Besides they offered to help with anything they needed help on.

Sammy Bradshaw and Shirley Lassen with the American Advertising Firm had a meeting scheduled with Jack Clayton, Vice President of Sales and Beth Johnson, Media Coordinator for Chevrolet Division of General Motors at nine that morning.

Sammy and Shirley burst into the conference room with such exciting news Sammy almost couldn't contain himself, in fact before he even sit down he started talking,

"Jack, Beth we got a great idea for weeks and weeks of free publicity, publicity you couldn't buy if you tried."

Jack said, "OK Sammy, what's your fabulous idea?"

"The road race for nineteen fifties vintage sports car from Moscow to Beijing!"

"Just what's that going to do for Chevrolet?"

"What's it going to do? I'll tell you what it's going to do. It's going to get you of the front page of every newspaper in America and half of the world."

"I haven't heard of any road race in the world that creates that much excitement that every newspaper in the country will have it on their front page, much less for weeks."

"It just came off the newswire a few minutes ago, two Americans are entering the race with a nineteen fifty-eight Corvette."

"OK, so you got two Americans entering their old Vet in the race?"

"Not just two Americans, these Americans are lookers, one looks like Brad Pitt and the other one, Tom Cruise.

They don't just look like movie stars for God's sake, their nuclear scientists. A few years ago the government wouldn't have let these two guys anywhere near Russia and China, now they're going to be running a car race there."

"You got to be kidding?"

"No, I not kidding, Chevrolet got to provide them with a support team to help them the same way Jaeger and Mercedes and the other factories are doing for their cars and we're going to send Curtis La Salle, our top TV Producer and his cameraman,

PJ Murphy to film every step of the way for a documentary to be shown around the world.

"Jack you got a great opportunity with this story."

"OK, let's do it."

Beth said, "Jack, I think it's a great idea, but we need to get somebody with a certain charm and good looks to be the team leader, maybe a woman, but I guess she needs to know something about Corvettes."

Sammy replied, "Great idea Beth, maybe you've got a good looking young Black Woman who looks like Halle Berry, now that would make terrific press."

Jack picked up a phone and called the head of Engineering, George Wilde and asked him if he knew if he had a young engineer in his

Department who knew a lot about Corvettes, especially the old ones from the fifties, who could be sent on a special assignment?"

"I've got a young woman that's nuts over Vets and her dad is a mechanic who taught her all about them when she was growing up. She's got an Engineering Degree in Automotive Design from the University of Michigan.

"She's one of the brightest young engineers in my Department, but I guess she could be made available for a special project. How long would you want her?"

"A couple months, well maybe three months."

"Yes, I remember the last time you wanted one of my people for a few months and I haven't seen him for twenty years, except in meetings or in the hallways of the office complex. I don't trust you borrowing my people for a few months."

"I promise I'll give her back to you."

"All right Jack, I'll send her in to see you."

"George, could you have her come to Conference Room One, right now, it's kind of important."

"Yeah, I know what you do is important and what we do is nothing, but I'll have her come to see you right away."

Ten minutes past before they heard a knock on the conference room door and Beth opened the door and Annie Taylor entered the room.

She wasn't Halle Berry, but she was Black and Beautiful and looked terrific in her white jumpsuit.

Jack couldn't believe it and Sammy was thrilled, Annie Taylor was perfect for what they wanted, he only hoped she knew the front end of a Vet from the back end.

"I'm Annie Taylor, Mr. Wilde asked me to meet with Mr. Clayton."

Jack told her he was Jack Clayton and introduced her to the rest of the folks in the room.

Then he said, "I understand from George you know quite-a-bit about old Corvettes, say from the nineteen fifties is that right?"

"I grew up with them, my dad was one of the top mechanics on those models and he had me by his side, since I was five years old helping him work on them."

"You sound like the perfect person for a special assignment for me, if you like those old cars."

"No, I wouldn't say I like them, more like I loved them."

"You're perfect we want you to be the team leader for a Chevrolet sponsored Corvette that's running in the Moscow to Beijing Road Race."

"When is this race and how long would I be away from home?"

"I would say you'd be gone for about three months and the race starts about four months from today."

"Is it all right with Mr. Wilde, if I'm gone that long?"

"I spoke with him about it and he gave me the OK not only that, but if you do a good job and help these guys win the race. I'll get you promoted and you'll head up the design team for a brand new Corvette."

"Can you do that?"

"I can do it."

"OK, when do I start?"

Sammy said, "You don't know it young lady, but we're going to make you a TV star too, because we're going to film every step of this trip for a documentary."

Jack said, "Annie welcome aboard, the project is now in your hands and if you run into any roadblocks call me, and I'll have them moved."

"Thank you for this opportunity Mr. Clayton, I won't let you down."

"I'm sure you won't, good luck.

"Sammy will fill you in on the name of the owners of the car and all of the details about the race."

"Sammy explained who owned the car and who the drivers were and the one little detail that hadn't been exactly worked out yet.

"Like they hadn't contacted the car owner, Dr. Chance Taylor and offered to provide factory support to him and his car for the race."

Annie couldn't believe it, however she would find out a lot more things she couldn't believe before this assignment was over.

Sammy suggested Annie call and talk, to Dr. Chance Taylor and offer to provide factory assistance for the race to him, as Sammy said, men have a hard time saying no to a woman.

Annie tried to contact Dr. Taylor at Sandia, but was told Sandia policy didn't allow personal calls to employees.

She tried getting his home number, but there was no telephone number listed for Chance Taylor in Albuquerque, so then she tried Charles V. Brown, no listing for him either.

Sandia didn't allow home numbers being listed for their scientists.

Sammy pulled some strings with one of the Albuquerque TV stations and they got Chance Taylor's home number through the police department.

Later in the evening Annie got Dr. Chance Taylor on the telephone and pitched the idea of a Chevrolet support team for his car at no cost and they would pay all of his expenses for the trip and even pay him and Dr. Charles Brown for allowing them to film all of their experiences running the race.

Chance found it hard to say no to the deal, so he said yes.

Annie asked him to tell her all about his Corvette, so she could have everything ready for the race, even if they had to completely rebuild the car during the race.

Chance told her about his Corvette was a 1958 with a 290-horsepower Rochester fuel injection V-8 engine; four speed manual transmission; heavy duty racing suspension; the color of his car was Regal Turquoise, with the side cove painted white and with a dark grey interior; auxiliary hardtop; and power operated folding top.

He had Goodyear white side wall tires, size 6.70 x 15 mounted on his car.

Annie told him she would begin to assembly a team to meet them in Europe with everything from a new engine; transmission and rear end and everything in between.

She would be in Albuquerque in two weeks to go over the car from front to back and pack it for shipping.

Chance told her he had made arrangements to send the car by ship from New Orleans to Odessa.

Annie said, "OK, I'll make arrangements to have the team meet us in Odessa to transport it and us to Moscow."

Chance said fine, "I was just going to drive it there."

Annie replied, "We will be doing everything first class from now on."

Chance said, "That's OK with me."

Chance suddenly had an entourage of six people with him: Charles; Anmend; Kerida; Annie Taylor; Curtis La Salle and PJ Murphy, not exactly what he envisioned a week ago.

He wasn't certain why Chevrolet wanted to sponsor his car, but figured they wanted to use him for publicity, so he guessed it would be OK if he used them to help him win the race.

He would make arrangements for four staterooms on the freighter. He didn't know if they could give them four staterooms or not, if so; he would put Charles in with him; Kerida and Annie together: Curtis and PJ together and Anmend in a room by himself.

Chance was able to make the arrangements for the staterooms, but the shipping company told him he booked all of the staterooms they had available for the trip.

Charles was impressed to hear Chevrolet would be sponsoring them in the race and shooting a TV film about their trip and paying them.

Two weeks later, Annie Taylor arrived in Albuquerque to check over the Corvette and make it ready for the long ocean voyage.

Chance was very impressed with her knowledge of his car and impressed with her in general. He thought she had a sharp wit, good sense of humor and was very nice to look at.

Annie told him Curtis La Salle and PJ Murphy would be arriving tomorrow to be available to shoot filming of her checking-out the car before it was packed for shipment.

Annie told him she would wrap the car with a covering to protect it from the ocean air.

GM was sending a plane to fly them and the car to New Orleans for their trip to Odessa.

Everything was ready, all of the travelers had their passports and visas for all of the countries they would be visiting on the trip.

Annie had uniforms made for everyone going on the trip with their names on them and the Corvette Logo.

The driver's helmets were stenciled the same way, along with baseball caps embroidered with the Corvette Logo on them to wear when they weren't wearing their racing helmets.

Chance thought they sure looked like a professional race team even if they weren't.

The car and crew were now taking the first step on their long journey; they were enroute to New Orleans on a General Motors plane.

2

Chance, Charles, Anmend, Kerida and Annie Taylor descend the stairs from the GM jet and watched as they begin unloading the Corvette out of the storage compartment of the plane.

A limo was waiting to pick them up to take them to the Cornstalk Hotel in the French Quarter in New Orleans.

Curtis La Salle, TV Producer and his cameraman, PJ Murphy, were waiting for their arrival.

They had taken a commercial flight earlier to have time to film the ship, which would be carrying the race car to Europe and to have things ready to film the arrival of the team on the GM jet and the unloading of the car from the plane.

Annie told everyone before they went to the hotel; they first had to accompany the Corvette, down to the dock, where it was to be loaded onto the ship, the Panama Star.

Chance looked at his beloved car all wrapped-up to protect it from the ocean air and thought it looked awful, like someone who had been injured and was being held together with plastic wrap and foam.

His baby didn't look very beautiful wrapped up like that, but Annie assured him it was to provide the protection it needed from the salt air. Even the bottom of the car and engine had been wrapped with a plastic wrap to protect it from rust.

The Corvette was loaded onto the bed of a wrecker truck to transport it to the ship. Annie stood next to the driver of the wrecker giving him instructions on being careful loading the car and securing the car for its ride to the ship.

She told the driver she had the Vet in perfect condition for the road race and she didn't want it damaged in any way getting it there.

11

Soon they were all in the limo following the truck with the Corvette, except for Curtis and PJ who had their own car and were filming the car been transported through the New Orleans traffic.

Annie was in the front seat with the driver urging him to stay up with the vehicle carrying Chance's car.

Chance commented, "Annie said we would be going first class with Chevrolet footing the bill and she doing everything possible to see we do."

After they arrived at the dock, Annie met with the Captain of the Panama Star and gave him the papers for shipping the Corvette.

After she and Chance saw the car was securely on the ship and locked in place and the filming done of the car being loaded and safely stored for its ocean voyage they were ready to check into their hotel.

The Captain told them they would be sailing tomorrow afternoon around four and they should plan to be onboard between two-thirty and three.

After they checked into the hotel, Annie told everyone she had made reservations for dinner at Antoine's at eight and planned to have breakfast tomorrow morning at Café Du Monde.

Tonight, they would each have a room by themselves, one last luxury before bunking with someone else for the ocean voyage, except Anmend who would have his own room on the ship.

The Panama Star was not a luxury liner, but a true ocean going freighter with only four passenger cabins.

Chance had heard about Antoine's all his life, but had never eaten there, so he was looking forward to dinner and he loved beignets at Café Du Monde.

They weren't going to be in New Orleans very long, but they were certainly going to be well fed before leaving on their trip.

Dinner at Antoine's was fantasy and by the time they finished three or four bottles of French Champagne, no one was feeling any pain. Next, they were ready for some New Orleans Jazz and Cajun Music.

They spend the next four hours listening to the music that makes New Orleans, New Orleans. What a wonderful time they were having and no one except Charles and Kerida were ready to leave to go to bed.

Finally, the others told them to go on and they would meet them in the morning at eleven. Anmend asked his sister, if she was feeling all right, she assured him she was just tired.

When Charles and Kerida returned to the hotel they went to Kerida room and were soon in each other's arms and making love.

This would be one of the few times they would be able to spend a whole night together and they intended to make the most of it, who knew when they would have an opportunity like this again.

The rest of the party returned to their rooms around four in the morning and by eleven the next morning they were all in the lobby ready to go.

Kerida came to the lobby looking as she had never gone to bed, put nicely she looked awful.

When Charles hadn't appeared by then, Chance called his room and got no answer.

About the time Chance returned from making his call, Charles arrived looking in worse condition then Kerida.

Chance said to the group, "I'm glad we didn't come back early, the way these two look, you would have thought they never went to bed."

Neither, Kerida, nor Charles bothered to respond.

Little did Chance or the others have any idea of the night Kerida and Charles had, they went to bed all right, but sleeping was not on their agenda.

They had far more important things on their minds.

Everyone enjoyed the beignets at Café Du Monde, but no one as much as Chance who had four or was it six, after while he quit counting.

After finishing the beignets they went back to the hotel to repack and checked-out since their limo was scheduled to pick them up at two.

By three o'clock everyone had their luggage stored in their staterooms and out on the deck watching as the Panama Star preparing to get under way.

Captain Jack Black was giving orders and watching his crew respond. He had an experienced crew who'd worked with him before, so they knew what he expected and knew the ship.

A few minutes before four in the afternoon the Panama Star left its berth and was underway for a very long voyage, with the first port of call more than a week away at Madeira Island off the coast of Africa.

After a day and a half in Madeira, the ships next stop three days later would be in Gibraltar, where they would stay for two days; one extra stop had been added to their trip a stop in Sicily for a day: then on to Istanbul; and finally their destination, Odessa.

Curtis and PJ had gotten wonderful footage of each stop of the racing team enjoying the local sights and the shots on the ocean voyage on the Panama Star were perfect.

Curtis knew he had an award winning documentary.

Traveling on a working freighter was not exactly like making a Trans Atlantic voyage on the QE II, there was no cruise director seeing to ever need of their passengers; no entertainment show nightly; and certainly no six meals a day, no they had three meals a day with the crew.

The passengers passed through a chow line just like a crew member and the only women aboard where Kerida and Annie.

The funny thing was all of the passengers seemed to be enjoying the trip, just watching the crew going about their daily tasks and the work of loading and unloading the ship in each port.

In short they all were having a real experience.

Everything was going well and right on schedule as the ship left Istanbul for Odessa.

All of the passengers had fully enjoyed the trip and were looking forward to their arrival in Odessa for the last phase of their journey to Moscow.

Annie had been in communications with her Chevrolet Support Team, they were waiting for her in Odessa.

Chance was getting anxious to start the long road race from Moscow to Beijing.

In fact all of his group was ready to win the big race and were really looking forward to getting started.

Only Annie was concerned, she was worrying about something happing to the car that she hadn't thought of and she wouldn't have the parts to fix it.

She talked to her father at length about his thoughts of potential problem parts for a nineteen fifty-eight Corvette over a long road race and had all of those parts made and on hand in one of the support trucks, these parts were in addition to the ones she had chosen.

Plus, she had spoken to some of the retired engineers who were still living who had worked on the design and building of the "58" Vets.

She added parts they suspected might be a problem to her in her inventory of spare parts.

She thought she had enough spare parts traveling with them on the race that she could build a second car if she had too.

Around four o'clock in the morning, Chance and Charles were awoken by a loud noise on the main deck of the ship.

Chance could hear a lot of shouting and then the sounds of gunfire.

Chance jumped straight out of bed and grabbed his clothes he had taken off the night before. Charles was not far behind him. Both of them ran to the main deck to see what was going on.

What they saw was some type of patrol boat with a Romanian Flag. The men on the boat were dressed in uniforms and several others were standing on the deck of the Panama Star.

They were shocked to see Captain Jack Black had been shot and was lying on the deck with blood pour from his chest.

The sailor who had been steering the ship was sitting on the floor of the pilot house with two men standing over him with guns pointing at his head.

As others members of the crew came up on deck the uniformed men were forcing them to their knees and putting their arms behind their back and placing plastic straps around their wrist.

One of the uniformed men asked Chance in English, where the rest of his party was.

Chance told them he thought they must be in their staterooms.

Two of the raiding party took hold of him, and shoved him in the direction of the staterooms.

Chance had no choice, but to lead the men to the staterooms.

Arriving at Anmend stateroom room they smashed in the door as Anmend was putting on his pants.

One of the men grabbed Anmend and pulled him out of the room into the hall where Chance and the other raider were standing.

Next, they approached the stateroom of Kerida and Annie, again one of the men smashed open the door both of the women were dressed and were crouching behind one of the beds.

The man motioned to the women to come out of the room and when Kerida hesitated to move to the door right away, the man who had entered the room slapped her so hard she fell to the floor.

He grabbed her by the arm as Chance tried to go to her aid, but instead of being able to help her. He was rewarded with a pistol hitting him in the back of his head.

Chance fell to the floor and the raider who had hit Chance told Anmend in English to help him up.

Anmend reach down and put both of his arms under Chance's arms and help pull him to an upright position.

Next, came the room of Curtis and PJ, both of them were dressed and had opened the door and coming to see what the problem was.

They soon found out what the problem, as one of the raiders stuck a automatic rifle into Curtis stomach and told him to march up the stairs with the others.

The six of them were lead up to the main deck where by now all of the crew members of the ship were down on their knees; their hands strapped behind them and all facing the outside wall of the ship.

All of the seven captives had their wrist bound behind them with the plastic straps.

Next, the raiders transfer the two women over to their boat: then Charles; next Anmend; then Curtis and PJ.

The last one to be transferred was Chance, and as he was being taken across the plank that the raiders had placed between their boat and the Panama Star.

Suddenly a gust of wind and a large wave rocked the plank and Chance and the raider taking him across, were thrown into the sea.

The raider was able to grab hold of the plank, as the end which had been on the ship hit the water and his companions managed to grab the other end of the plank on their boat and pulled it and the raider out of the water.

The raiders couldn't see Chance in the water and tried shinning bright lights on the water, but Chance was nowhere to be seen.

The leader of the raiders was really upset about losing Chance, during the transfer from the ship to their boat and screaming at his men.

The raiders replaced the plank back between their boat and the ship and prepared to take the remaining raiders on the ship onboard their boat, but before they did.

They systematically shot each of the crew members in the back of their head.

With that task completed, the rest of the raiders returned to their boat.

The raiders started up the engines on their boat and after they were about a half a mile away from the ship they blew a large hole on the port side of the ship.

A few minutes later, a second large explosion came and pieces of the ship were blown in all directions.

After the boat had traveled for about an hour, the raiders guided their boat into a small dock.

They secured the boat to the dock and removed their passengers, and then they covered the boat with a camouflage tarp, and placed tree branches over the tarp.

The hostages were placed on a bus and as soon as all of the raiders but two were on the bus, the bus pulled out onto a small paved road.

After a few minutes, the bus came to a highway not much wider than the road they just came off of.

Both of the women were softly crying; Curtis and PJ sat looking stunned; and Charles and Anmend were trying to keep up their courage by looking at each other, in disbelieve at what had happened to them.

They wanted to say something to try to give courage to the others and to themselves, but the raiders had told them to keep their mouths shut or they would be gagged.

As daylight began to break, the hostages could see mountains in the distance and their bus was moving as quickly as it could toward them.

It took another hour and half for the bus to reach the foothills of the mountains, shortly after that the bus began climbing a long curvy highway at an about a forty degree angle up the mountain.

The driver had to start down shifting gears to keep up any speed; the bus started chugging like it was going to stop. The driver continued to down shift gears until the bus was in its lowest gear.

Charles thought to himself, he could have almost walked as fast as the bus was now traveling. Then he thought about Chance, and watching him slip into the sea with his hands tied behind him.

He couldn't believe he was gone, they had been together for so long and just like that, he was gone.

After another hour of climbing, the bus came to a small lane and turned onto it. The lane was very rocky and the bus was sliding from one side of the road to the other.

Charles thought unless you knew where the lane was when you approached it, you would have driven right by it.

Finally, he could see they were approaching a rather large house. When the bus stopped at the house, the hostages were instructed to get off.

By this time the women were no longer crying and a large bruise was visible on Kerida face, where she had been struck by the guard.

Anmend felt angry at the raider who struck her and wanted to attack him, but thought better of it since all of the guards were well armed and he remembered what happened to the crew on the ship.

He knew they would not hesitate to kill him.

The hostages were taken into the house and their plastic straps removed from their wrist.

A few minutes later the leader of the raiders, who had left them when they got on the bus came into the large living room where they were at.

He looked over the hostages and his men and told his men something in Arabic and they all left the room and went outside the house.

Then the leader said in English, "Good morning, I hope your bus ride was not too uncomfortable, my men should have taken your straps off of your wrists when you got on the bus.

My name is Dr. Abu al-Sadr. I will be your host during your stay at the Mountain Top Lodge. You're here for one purpose and that is to have Dr. Brown, do some work for me, which I will be talking to him about later.

Some of my people are searching for Dr. Taylor to either find him or his body.

Does anyone have any questions?"

Charles said, "If you only wanted me, why have you taken these other folks?"

"My good doctor, they give me insurance to be certain you do the work I want you to do."

Dr. al-Sadr spoke again, "We have one rule here during your stay, if you try to escape we will kill you and doctor if you don't do the work we want you to do, we will kill your friends, one at a time.

"We will not just kill them; they will be suffering so bad they will be begging us to finish killing them.

"I hope you understand we mean business and won't stand for any monkey business.

"You will be treated well, as long as you do exactly as we say, if not you will be treated very badly.

"Does everyone understand the rules for your stay with us?"

Each of the captives nodded their head in agreement and then Dr. al-Sadr said he would show them to their rooms.

Each of the captives had a room to themselves with a bath. In each room were clothes the size of each of the hostages.

The bathrooms were equipped with toilet items each of the captives might need. It was very obvious whoever planned this kidnapping knew everything about the people they were taking.

Dr. al-Sadr showed Charles to his room last, and then proceeded to explain exactly what he wanted him to do, assemble small nuclear bombs, which could be carried in suitcases.

He also told Charles it was too bad about losing Dr. Taylor, because he knew Charles needed him to make the triggers to fire the bombs. However, you will just have to muddle through without Dr. Taylor, as my British friends would say.

3

ank Sollenberger was in trouble again at the CIA after he return from another unauthorized trip he made for the past three weeks to Argentina and Brazil, he looking to confirm his theory al-Qaeda had rigged the last elections in both countries to obtain a foothold in the Americas.

He couldn't find anything to confirm his theory, nothing, no leads, not even a suspect. After three weeks there, no one would even consider such a thing, even the most radical newspapers in the countries wouldn't consider it they just laughed at him.

Hank's immediate supervisor, Beverly Jenkins didn't laugh at all about him taking another unauthorized trip, chasing a theory no one else at CIA would even consider.

If she could, she would have terminated his employment with the CIA immediately.

However, as soon as she talked with the Deputy Director of the CIA, Ron Parsons, she was told she wouldn't be given authorization for the termination.

Ron told her he had a theory about Hank, one day one of his wild theories will turn out to be right and save a lot of American lives.

So after another verbal reprimand and one more notice added to the pile of reprimands in Hank's file, regarding his verbal reprimands for traveling without prior authorization.

He returned to his office as he saw the smug smiles and heard the soft laugher of his fellow analysts about his latest venture.

Being away for three weeks, his desk was piled high with newspapers from several countries, as well as all of the major U.S. newspapers and then there were the magazines stacked high on the floor next to his desk.

Anyway the mess in his office was like the mess in his mind, always thinking of several different things in four different languages at the same time. Sometimes four different languages, then the ones he was thinking about five minutes before.

It was no wonder Hank had such a hard time focusing on one thing, oh but when he did, then it was the only thing he could think about, no then he was obsessed with it.

The CIA had a brilliant man, as an analysts and theorist in Hank Sollenberger at twelve he graduated from high school and had three doctorates from Harvard, before he was twenty.

He could speak, write and read ten languages, including Russian and Mandarin Chinese; he lacked only one thing, common sense.

Hank had grown up with a father and mother who were too old when he was born and both of them were university professors of foreign languages, who taught him how to read in six languages, before he started to kindergarten.

Hank was indeed unique, not just unique, but scary to his fellow workers, he would be speaking to them in English and then go off into two other languages to finish his sentence.

Recently, Hank moved out of his apartment in Rockville, Maryland into his CIA office because he determined his place was bugged and even though he had it swept for bugs by the CIA; and they found nothing.

He knew al-Qaeda or maybe it was Castro who was out to kill him.

Why would he think Castro was out to kill him, because Hank once put forth the theory the Castro Government was part of the 9-11 plot and someone in the CIA leaked the story and the local Washington Newspapers, picked up the story and printed it on their front pages under headlines reading "CIA Suspects Castro Behind 9-11 Attack."

The newspapers saying a CIA senior analyst has strong suspicions Castro helped plan the attacks on the Pentagon and the World Trade Centers.

The true story behind the headlines came from one of Hank's fellow analyst's who told a friend about the crazy idea one of their analyst came up, which had everyone at CIA laughing in stitches about it.

They thought it was one of the funnies things they had ever heard. However, as the story traveled around the beltway, the joke at CIA became a real theory by the time the story made its way to the newspapers.

Hank was now home safely in his office at CIA Headquarters in Langley, Virginia and he was back reading his newspapers, left over from the last three weeks.

He started with the American ones first and after reading through those and finding nothing of interest; he read all of the Herald Tribune's; next he started on the French newspapers, from them he went to the Russian newspapers.

In the back of one of the Russian newspapers, he found a story about an unconfirmed rumor of a break-in at one of Russian nuclear weapons facility, which perked his interest.

However, the director of the facility and the government both denied the story. Hank carefully cut out the story and pinned it on his cork board behind his desk.

One name caught his eye in the story, Colonel Zaro Zmitrovitch, with Russian Intelligent who was named as the officer in charge of the investigation.

Hank recognized his name as being one of Russian most notorious KGB agents from the cold war period.

Hank thought it would be important to have field agents in Russia follow-up on the reported break-in to see if they could find out if there was any true in the story.

Hank sent a request to Moscow to see what the local agents could find out about this incident.

Two days later, the CIA Moscow Bureau reported there seemed to be too much denial for there not to be some true to the story.

No one was talking and rumors were beginning to come to light, there may have been a cover up of the incident. Most of the information they were able to glean seems to indicate someone may have broken into one of the nuclear facilities, but nothing of any value was taken.

This report caused Hank to be sure something was going on, just what he didn't know, but something was going on. He decided not to talk to anyone about it, without having a better theory then he had at this moment.

A month passed, without anything else causing him suspicions of anything to the reported break-in in a Russia nuclear facility. Until he saw in the back of the Washington Post, a small story about two nuclear scientists employed by Sandia National Laboratory in Albuquerque, New Mexico reported missing after a freighter sank in the Black Sea, both presumed dead, since there were no survivors found.

Hank clipped this story out of the paper and put it up next to the story from the Russian newspaper. He had to find out who these men were and what they were doing on a freighter on the Black Sea.

He quickly contacted the newspaper in Albuquerque to see what information they had on the reported missing scientists from Sandia.

He was able to get the editor in charge of local news on the line and told him he was a freelance writer for the Washington Times and he was trying to put a human interest story about the two missing nuclear scientists who worked at Sandia.

The editor told him he was surprised Hank hadn't see some of the stories in the papers about the two nuclear scientists traveling to Russia with their 1958 Corvette to participate in the Moscow to Beijing Road Race.

Hank was surprised too, he hadn't seen the stories, but when he found out most of the stories had been on the sports pages of the newspapers, he understood how he missed the stories.

He never read the sports pages, sports were dumb. The editor said there had been a lot of TV coverage about them entering the race as well. Hank didn't watch TV either, not only didn't he watch TV, but he never owned a TV.

The editor told him Sandia announced yesterday they had received word from the sponsor of the car, Chevrolet of the sinking of the ship from the racing teams European support team, who had been waiting in Odessa for the ship to arrive.

The port authority in Odessa reported they had not received an SOS from the ship or anything, but after the ship didn't arrive, they checked with the Istanbul Port Authority and was told the Panama Star left there several days ago bound for Odessa.

Odessa sent out search vessels, but the only thing they found was debris from the ship including parts from one of the lifeboats.

The searchers concluded the ship blew-up, before anyone could escape, since the lifeboat was in pieces. No survivors were found only several empty life jackets.

The editor gave Hank the name of the scientists; Dr. Chance Taylor and Dr. Charles V. Brown, both of them were thirty-five.

Chance was never married and Charles wife's name was Cheryl and they had two children. The wife had been staying with her parents in Winnetka, Illinois at the time of the accident.

Hank's next call was to Chevrolet Headquarters to talk to someone about the car and the people they were sponsoring in the Moscow to Beijing Road Race.

His call was put through to Beth Johnson, Media Consultant. She told Hank, Chevrolet was providing the race team with complete support for the race, including having their advertising firm filming every aspect of the race including the trip to Russia by ship.

Beth said Annie Taylor a Chevy Engineer was in charge of the support team and was traveling along with Curtis La Salle and PJ Murphy, award winning producer and cameraman onboard the ship that sank as well as Dr. Chance Taylor and Dr. Charles Brown.

She said we have been trying to obtain more details about the problem with the ship, but so far we have been unable to get any more details except they think the ship sank off of the coast of Romania, somewhere between Istanbul and Odessa.

After talking with Beth Johnson, Hank sent a request to Istanbul CIA requesting them to obtain any information they could regarding a ship that sunk in the Black Sea enroute to Odessa from Istanbul.

He contacted Lloyds of London to see if they had a ship they insured which had been reported sank in the Black Sea in the past few days, indeed they did.

The ship was a freighter by the name of Panama Star, owned by the White Line Shipping Company, with headquarters in New Orleans and registered in Panama.

Hank called the White Line Shipping Company, using the same story he told all of the others he contacted about the ship, he was a freelance writer for the Washington Times.

His call was put through to Jacque French, who told him the Panama Star sailed from New Orleans with its first stop on the island of Madeira; then Istanbul and then Odessa.

The ship had a full load of cargo and seven passengers in four cabins, which was all of the cabins available.

Hank asked for the names of the passengers and he was told the passenger list by cabins were Dr. Chance Taylor and Dr. Charles V. Brown; Annie Taylor and Kerida Soekarmo; Curtis La Salle and PJ Murphy and Anmend Soekarmo.

Hank needed to find out whom, Kerida and Anmend Soekarmo were?

He requested information from the FBI, to see if they had any information on them and was shocked to find a whole file.

The file stated they were twins from Indonesia and their Grandfather was President Sukarno, Hank thought to himself he should have remembered the other spelling for Sukarno, sometime used in Indonesia was Soekarmo.

Both of the twins had applied for student visas and attended the University of Chicago, graduating the same year as Chance Taylor and Charles V. Brown.

Taylor and Brown went on to get their doctorate as Nuclear Physics and Kerida her doctorate in Languages. She was a professor at the University of New Mexico in Albuquerque.

Anmend had his Master's Degree from the University of Chicago in Political Science and taught there. Both had become citizens of the USA.

After checking with some of the colleagues of Anmend at the University of Chicago, he was told Anmend and Dr. Charles Brown had been college roommates for the four years, while they attended the University.

They were close friends and he and his sister had gone on the trip to help Chance and Charles with the race.

Talking with people on the phone at the University of New Mexico, Hank was told Kerida and her brother were very close and having the chance to spend a couple of months together on this road race would give them a wonderful opportunity to just be together.

Besides, she was fluent in both Russia and Mandarin Chinese, which would help the race team.

With that information Hank concluded the four of them were close friends and had a real desire to just go and win the road race for America and have a goodtime together.

Hank ran a credit check on all four of the missing friends and the woman who worked for Chevrolet: Dr. Chance Taylor, had an excellent credit report and owed only on his home, also his parents were wealthy; Dr. Charles V. Brown, was another story, he and his wife were living pay check to pay check, with bills way over their head, his parents were deceased, but her parents were multi-millionaires developers.

The Soekarmo were very well off with income and investments far exceeding their salaries, both with excellent credit.

Annie Taylor had excellent credit, although she was still paying on her college loans and a house, she had bought for her parents, but without any problems meeting her obligations.

Hank concluded being single gave you a better opportunity to save and manage your money and to stay out of debt.

Since, the only one of the group who had any real money problems and large debts was Dr. Charles Brown and he was the only one of the group who was married.

Hank checked on the security clearance for Drs. Taylor and Brown with both the FBI and Sandia, both of the men had the highest class of clearance needed for their type of work.

Sandia told him Dr. Taylor was the leading expert on triggers for nuclear weapons in America and Dr. Brown was one of the top researcher in miniaturize nuclear weapons.

Losing both of them had created a huge hole with their nuclear research and caused new policies to be written at Sandia about allowing two scientists to go on vacation or leave together.

The next bit of information to cross Hank's desk which perked his interest was increased traffic by al-Qaeda regarding some major project.

Much of this traffic was coming from the Middle East and Eastern Europe. This really peaked Hank's interest.

Why were they getting traffic from an area they seldom heard anything about from al-Qaeda, in Eastern Europe?

Hank began to formulate an idea; a scenario, what if somehow the nuclear scientists didn't go down on the Panama Star, but were kidnapped by al-Qaeda and instead of the breakin of the nuclear facility in Russia, who reported nothing was lost of any value.

Had in reality, had bomb making materials stolen from it and al-Qaeda had the materials to build nuclear weapons.

If al-Qaeda had the material and the scientist capable of assembling nuclear weapons what would they do with them and how would they get American Scientists to build the bombs?

Hank made copies of all of the items he had been collecting regarding his scenario and took it to meet with his supervisor, Beverly Jenkins.

Hank described his scenario to her in great detail and managed to do the whole presentation only in English.

Beverly rolled her eyes back in her head and when he finished. She chose her words carefully and said, "Hank your scenario is very interesting and I think you should continue to search for some solid information which could substantiate your theory.

"You got to obtain solid evidence to help me take this scenario to my superiors. Find me something to help prove your scenario. OK?"

An hour later everyone in his department was laughing about another crazy theory by Hank Sollenberger.

Hank realized he had to be right, but this time he intended to prove it if it was the last thing he did!

4

Chance felt the cold of the water, as he went under and the ache in his head where he had been hit with the pistol a few minutes ago. The coldest of the water awaken all of his senses and he realized what just happened to him.

With his awaking came the realization his life was in peril from drowning, since his wrists were bounded behind him.

Funny things come to the mind when your life is being threatened, a voice in his head keep repeating "Houston we got a problem" over and over. Chance realized it was he who had the problem and he had to get free of the plastic straps around his wrists, but how?

He was amazed to find in the water he was able to get into a fetal position and get his arms over his feet, so now he had his arms in front of him.

Next problem, he needed air, using his arms to help thrust himself up he started to ascend up in the water. When he came up near the surface of the water, he found he was under the rear of the raiders boat, from where he was at he could just make out the boat's propellers and worked his way back to where they were and came up for air.

He could hear men yelling and saw lights shining on the water in front of his position. He knew they were looking for him. He stayed as quiet as he could.

Then he went back under the boat to find the boat's propellers and tried to use one of them to cut through the plastic straps between his wrists. He was making a little progress, but found he was soon out of air again and had to resurface.

When he surfaced the second time he could hear gunfire. He repeated his trip a third time and on this trip his wrists were free from the plastic straps.

As he started back up to the surface for air he saw the propellers begin slowly turning, he quickly changed his direction away from the boat's propellers as they begin turning faster.

The boat started moving and made a left turn away from the ship and the boat almost ran over him as he swan as hard as he could to get away from it. Chance could see the boat was pulling away from the ship at a high rate of speed.

He saw the ship in the distance behind him and as he was trying to reverse the direction he had been swimming, he was tossed up in the air by the wake from the boat.

Chance again found himself submerged under the sea, he fought his way back to the surface, he reached the surface just as another wake pushed him farther away from the ship and then another and another, until he was farther away from the ship then he had ever been.

Finally, the wakes subsided and he was swimming back toward the ship and then he heard an explosion from the ship and he could see the Panama Star begin to sink, as it was sinking, a second explosion came and this time pieces of the ship were sent high in the air.

Pieces of the ship begin falling all around him and he had to duck to keep from being hit by some of the debris.

Chance could see the remains of the hull of the Panama Star slipping into a watery grave taking whatever was left onboard with her, including his beloved Corvette.

Chance didn't have time to spend worrying about a car. He had to get help and try to save his friends, from who knew what.

A large piece of a wooden shipping crate struck him on the head and he grabbed onto it and after considerable struggle he managed to pull himself upon it.

He started paddling using the wooden crate like a surf board in the direction the boat went carrying his friends.

Several hours after daylight came. Chance could see land and tried to propel his piece of shipping crate even faster toward it. As he got closer to the shore the waves help push him there.

When Chance finally waded ashore, he looked at his watch and found it was two in the afternoon and he didn't have any idea of where he was and he certainly didn't see any friendly natives waiting for him on his arrival.

All he could see was rocks and trees, no people; no town; no nothing. After he made his way through the brush that was near the shoreline he could see a small paved road.

He was dripping wet even though he had almost completely dried off in the hot sun during his shipping crate ride to the shore, but he got soaked again wading ashore.

He didn't know which way he should go, right or left and he didn't know if the people who had taken him captive were somewhere near by looking for him or not.

Chance heard a vehicle coming and decided he better hide since he didn't know who was in the vehicle. He quickly lay on the ground under a small bushy tree out of sight.

He had been right to hide, because he saw men dressed in the same uniforms the raiders wore and carrying automatic weapons, then he knew they were looking for him.

They were looking for him all right, but not very hard. Since they believed he couldn't have survived his fall in the water with his hands secured behind his back, no, they were convinced he drowned.

They were driving along the beach road, because their leader Dr. al-Sadr told them to, but they were sure he was wrong to think anyone could have made it alive to the shore and thought it would take weeks for his body to wash ashore, if it ever did.

However, being good foot soldiers, they would continue patrolling the beach road for as long as Dr. al-Sadr wanted them to.

After the vehicle past, he quickly got up and headed back toward the shoreline and begin walking in the same direction the raider's vehicle had gone, he thought maybe his friends were being held somewhere near here.

Chance continued walking along the beach until he could see a bunch of people on the beach ahead of him maybe a quarter-of-a-mile away.

He hoped they had not seen him as he made his way back into the trees and brush.

He continue along this direction hoping he could get close enough to see who these people were and if they could help him.

He slowly approached the sound of people talking and playing music. He lay down in a prone position and using his elbows crawled slowly up to the camp.

What he saw were women cooking; children running and playing in the water and several men playing musical instruments.

All seemed to be having a good time and there were none of them dressed in the uniforms of the raiders who attacked them.

Chance was trying to decide if he should get up and walk into their camp and ask for help when he felt a stick poking him in the back, when he turned he saw it wasn't a stick, but a rifle barrel.

The man holding the rifle motioned for him to get up off the ground. Chance did what he was told. The man with the rifle motioned for him to walk toward the camp.

Arriving in the center of the camp an older man approached him and started speaking to him in a language Chance couldn't understand. Chance turned up his hands and shrugged his shoulders and said "American."

Another young man came forward who spoke English and asked, "You are an American?"

"Yes, I'm an American."

The young man then said, "Who are you and what are you doing here?"

"My name is Chance Taylor and I escaped from some people who kidnapped me and my friends off of a ship on our way to Odessa."

"So, where are your friends?"

"I don't know."

"How did you get away from these men?"

"When they were taking me from the ship to their boat I fell into the sea and they thought I'd drown. Then the ship blew up and I found a piece of a wooden crate and floated on it to shore."

Then the young man told the rest of the people what Chance had told him. Then he said, "My name is Michael and we're Gypsies, our camp is not far from here. We came last night to play in the water and fish."

"Have you seen some men dressed in uniforms around here early this morning?"

"We saw some a few minutes ago passing by in a truck."

"Those are the men who kidnapped me and my friends."

Again Michael told the others what Chance said, by now they had all gather around this stranger who had been brought to their camp.

Chance asked "Can you help me find my friends or take me to a town where I could get some help?"

As Michael started to answer another man spoke to him and told him something Chance couldn't understand.

Michael then said, "Victor told me he saw a bus pass by with several men in uniform around five o'clock this morning and your friends could have been on the bus, but he didn't see them."

"Does he know which direction the bus went?"

"No."

Can you take me somewhere that I can get help?"

"If these men were in uniform I wouldn't want to trust any of the police or people around here if I was you."

"Are we in Romania?"

"Yes, we're in Romania."

"Could you take me to Bucharest, where I can talk with the American Embassy?"

"I'll ask my Kris."

Then Michael and the Kris of the Gypsies had a long discussion about taking Chance to Bucharest, before Chance got an answer to his question.

"My Kris says we can't take you to Bucharest right now."

"Why not, I have some money I could pay you?"

"It's not a question of money it's another problem, we recently left Bucharest because the police were trying to arrest several of our family members.

"What we can do is maybe help you find where your friends have been taken. We can give you food; drink; a safe place to stay and dry clean clothes. OK?"

"Can I speak to Kris, who is he?"

"The Kris is the leader of our family, like a chief, he only speaks Romany and he has already spoken and won't risk having our family members put in prison to help you.

"They would die in prison."

"OK, I understand and if that's the best help you can give. I'll accept the help you can give me, thank you."

"We maybe of more help then you think, we have a lot of eyes in this part of the country and maybe we can help you find your friends."

"Thank you, and thank your Kris for me."

A few more minutes past and another vehicle began approaching the Gypsy Camp, Michael put a hat and a scarf around Chance and had a beautiful young woman sit down on his lap.

The vehicle approached the camp very slowly and it had men in uniforms in it looking for Chance.

When the vehicle was directly in front of where Chance was sitting the young woman put her arms around his neck and begin kissing him, hiding his face from the men in the truck.

The men in the truck hooted and hollered at the lovers and then drove off.

As soon as the truck was gone Michael told Chance he could quit kissing the young woman, now except he hadn't told her to stop.

Then Michael screamed at her in Romany to quit kissing Chance.

She quit and Chance got a good look at her as she was getting up off of his lap, she was beautiful, like no woman he had ever known.

Flashing black eyes and long black hair and skin the color of an almond. She got off of his lap and gave a little swing of her skirt toward him.

Michael told Chance, the woman was his sister, Juanita and she is the biggest flirt around, but doesn't have one serious beau and she is getting very old for an unmarried Gypsy woman. Our women marry young or never.

After all of the family finished dinner they loaded all of their equipment and people then got into several vehicles and begin driving to their camp.

Chance was in the vehicle with Michael and his family and Juanita.

Michael told Chance his parents were dead and Juanita was the youngest one in the family and since he was the oldest he took her in with his wife and children.

They entered the same highway his friends had traveled earlier in the day and in the same direction, Chance just didn't know it.

They were soon climbing the same mountains the raiders had gone up and about halfway up the very steep mountain the lead vehicle of the Gypsy caravan turned off of the highway onto a small dirt road and all of the other cars in the caravan followed him.

Before much longer they arrived at the Gypsy Camp, their Chance saw several trailers and wagons, which had been fitted to be pulled by cars. Some of the wagons were beautifully decorated with paintings and markings of various kinds, others looked very plain.

Michael took Chance to his trailer, which was one of the better looking living quarters in the Gypsy Camp and was told it had belonged to his parents and when they died, since he was the oldest son, it was his.

Michael searched through some clothing and found a shirt and a pair of pants he thought Chance might be able to wear. He also gave him a pair of underwear from a drawer in the bedroom.

Chance took off his briefs and put on the underwear Michael had given him, then he tried on the pants and they fit him all right around the waist, but were about two inches too short in length.

Michael called Juanita to come and see what she could do with his pants.

Juanita took a pair of scissors and cut loose the hem which had been turned under the pant legs she marked the length with a piece of soap and told Chance to take off his pants.

Chance couldn't understand what she was telling him. So she reached up and unfastened his pants and began pulling them off.

Chance tried to resist, but she already had his pant legs down around his ankles, so he pulled the right pant leg over his right foot and then the left one over his left foot.

Chance was left standing there in the middle of the bedroom with only his borrowed underwear on, as Juanita sit down on the bed and begin hemming the pant legs.

After she finished sewing the pants, she heated an iron powered by an electric generator built into the trailer. When she had the pants pressed she handed them to Chance and he put them on.

Juanita turned to go and Chance told her, "Thank you."

Chance still had a very wet pair of deck shoes to dry off and his socks, the rest of his clothes Juanita picked up on her way out of the bedroom and said something he didn't understand.

Michael heard her as he was coming back into the bedroom and told Chance Juanita said she would wash his clothes for him.

Michael took him out of the trailer and showed him a lean-to tent attached to his trailer and told him he could sleep here.

He promised tomorrow they would see what they could do about finding where his friends were being held.

As Chance lay down on his cot he saw Juanita coming into his tent, she came directly to him and took out her scissors. Chance didn't know what he should do, she took hold of his right hand and cut the plastic bracelet off of his wrist then the left one, they had been left around his wrists after he managed to cut the plastic straps using the propeller of the boat.

Next, she leaned down and kissed him and left, but as she was leaving she said his name, "Chance."

Maybe Juanita couldn't speak English, but she could say his name.

He fell asleep thinking how lucky he was to be alive after the ordeals he had survived since four o'clock this morning.

He could only hope his friends had been as lucky.

5

ank Sollenberger continued monitoring every report and newspapers that came into CIA Headquarters from Russia to see if he could find anything more about the reported break-in at one of Russia's nuclear laboratories.

He couldn't find a scrap of news about the break-in either in the CIA Reports or the Russian newspapers.

Hank had spoken with Chance Taylor's parents and they knew nothing more then what had been reported in the newspaper about him being lost in the sinking of the Panama Star; same story with Charles Brown's wife.

He also talked with the Chevrolet people and Annie Taylor's parents; they didn't know any more than he did about the accident.

The representatives of Curtis La Salle and PJ Murphy just said they couldn't believe they were gone.

The representative of the White Shipping Line told Hank they recently had the Panama Star completely refurbished and safety inspected by the US Coast Guard.

They said the sinking of the Panama Star made no sense to them, all information they had was the seas were calm; no bad weather and an experienced captain and crew onboard.

The ship had been refitted with the latest radar and communication systems. They felt something had really gone wrong, since there wasn't even a distress signal sent out from the ship.

Hearing that, Hank's concept was reinforced the Panama Star just didn't sink, it was sunk by somebody. He contacted the US Coast Guard and got a copy of the inspection report.

After he read the report, he was more convinced than ever that Dr. Chance Taylor and Dr. Charles Brown were kidnapped to be used to construct nuclear weapons using whatever materials were taken from the Russian nuclear lab.

He still lacked any prove that one; the nuclear scientists were kidnapped and two; there was anything of value taken from the Russians.

Outside of that, he had a great theory, but not one shred of evidence that either event had taken place.

Hank's next move wasn't going to help his career at the CIA, he by passed Beverly Jenkins and went straight to Ron Parsons and told him his theory about the missing scientists and the break-in at the Russian lab and he knew these two events were connected and somebody had the scientists to have them construct nuclear bombs.

Ron listened to him very patiently, then told Hank he should never come to him without the approval of his supervisor.

He also told Hank, Beverly Jenkins discussed his concept with him several weeks ago when Hank first told her his theory about the missing scientists.

Ron said, "Hank, you need some kind of prove to backup your theory, and so far you don't have anything. I've read all of the reports from our agents in Russia and I haven't seen anything which leads me to believe your theory about nuclear material being stolen from any lab in Russia is true.

"I'm sorry Hank, but I just can't see there is anything to your theory."

"Mr. Parsons, I feel it in my gut that I'm right. I know I'm right. You just got to believe me, America is going to be a target for those nuclear devices being put together somewhere right now, using our scientists and stolen Russian nuclear material."

"Hank, you maybe be right, but I've got to have something more to go on besides your theory, you need prove, even if I knew you were right what can I do without a clue as to where these people are and what their plans are.

"I'll tell you what we can do, nothing!"

"Mr. Parsons, I'll keep working to find prove of my theory and figure out where this work is going on, and where our scientists are."

"OK Hank, you find me something that proves your theory and we'll do everything possible to find the American Nuclear Scientists."

Hank went back to his office and decided he wasn't going to get any prove of his theory sitting in his office at CIA Headquarters in Langley, Virginia.

He packed his briefcase and a few pieces of clothing in his suitcase.

Then he had a taxi take him to Dulles International Airport and found a flight leaving for Athens, with connections to Istanbul. He bought a ticket using his CIA credit card and was off to Istanbul.

Arriving in Istanbul the next afternoon he heard about an American salvage company working off of the Greek island of Samothrakl, exploring a Greek vessel sunk during the Trojan War.

The salvage company was well known to Hank, because they had been involved in helping to locate the Titanic. Hank hired a boat to take him to the site where the company was working.

Arriving at the site he managed to board the salvage ship and talked to the Director of Operations, Luke Turner. Hank explained he was with the CIA and showed him his CIA credentials and gave him his business card.

Hank told him he had an urgent matter of National Security and needed his help at once. Hank told Luke Turner the matter required them to find a freighter recently sunk in the Black Sea, enroute from Istanbul to Odessa with two American Nuclear Scientists onboard.

It was a matter of live and death of maybe millions of Americans to find out why this ship sank and if the two scientists' bodies could be found or if there was proof of terrorist's sinking the ship.

Hank assured Mr. Turner the American Government would pay him for all of the services necessary to locate the sunken ship.

Luke Turner told Hank it would take them the rest of the day to disengage from their current operation and come to Istanbul to meet him.

Hank told Luke that would be fine and he was staying at the Istanbul Hilton.

It was almost midnight when Luke Turner called to tell Hank they had arrived in Istanbul and would be ready to leave by four tomorrow morning and that he and his crew were staying aboard their ship overnight and would see him in the morning.

Hank was up and dressed by three am and checked out of the hotel and took a taxi to the dock where the Discovery II was docked.

It was only a few minutes to four when Hank went onboard the ship. True to his word, Luke Turner and his crew had the Discovery II underway by four.

Luke told Hank he had meet with several captains of freighters last night who regularly traveled to Odessa from Istanbul and they had shown him the normal sea lane most all of them took for the trip.

At least it gave them a general direction they should be traveling to search for the lost ship.

Hank had no idea of the sophisticated equipment the Discovery II had onboard to help them find a sunken ship and recover items from them.

All Hank knew, was he had read a report on the abilities of the ship to locate almost anything on the ocean floor. It was a miracle the Discovery II was in the area to be available to help him.

After three days of searching Luke and his crew believed they found the remains of the Panama Star, but it was getting too dark for them to start having their remote controlled mini sub loaded with cameras and other equipment to begin surveying the wreck site.

Hank could hardly contain himself in anticipation of what they would find. Luke told him they would be ready to start around eight in the morning,

Hank watched his watch all night long, he saw every hour from ten last night until seven this morning and most every minute in between. Finally, he got out of his bunk and went on deck to see the crew preparing the mini sub for its trip to the bottom of the sea.

As Hank watched, the mini sub was swung over the side of Discovery II and watched as it went under the water.

One of the crew members told Hank to go inside the operation room and he could watch on a television screen everything the mini sub saw.

Hank quickly went to the operations room to watch the TV monitor as Luke was operating the mini sub by remote control. Deeper and deeper the sub went; it was fascinating to watch the skills of Luke control the sub from this operations room.

At last the sub reached the bottom of the sea and Luke begin moving the sub closer to where sonar indicated the ship remains were located.

When the sub got close enough to the ship Luke said, "That's not our ship, it's an old German warship of some kind from World War II."

Hank asked, "Are you sure?"

"I'm sure looked at what's left of the gun turret; we don't have freighters with those on them."

It took the crew most of the rest of the day to recover the mini sub and clean it up and make it ready for its next use.

The Discovery II started another sweep of the area Luke believed the Panama Star would have been traveling if it was anywhere close to the normal shipping lanes.

Two more weeks past before Luke thought he may have located the Panama Star's remains. Hank was not as excited as he was the first time as he waited for the mini sub to begin its search of the bottom of the sea looking for the Panama Star.

Hank Sollenberger had been missing from his office for the past two weeks.

Beverly Jenkins became concerned he was off again on another wild goose chase trying to prove his theory of stolen nuclear material from Russia and missing American Nuclear Scientists, building bombs for terrorists somewhere in the world to target Americans.

Beverly had agents contact the airlines at Dulles to see if Hank had flown to Russia and someone else checking with the credit card company to see if he used his CIA credit card to buy an airline ticket.

The answer was yes, Hank purchased an airline ticket two weeks ago, but it wasn't to Russia it was to Istanbul.

Beverly could hardly wait to talk to Ron Parsons about Hank's unauthorized trip to Istanbul, this time she knew she had enough to fire him and get this nut case out of her hair.

Ron agreed he could no longer afford to have an undisciplined agent running all over the world trying to prove a theory, when he had no prove of any kind to support his theory.

Ron still wondered if he was doing the right thing authorizing the termination of Hank since he continued to have a feeling one day Hank would prove to be worth all of the trouble he had caused in the past for the CIA.

Ron told Beverly, she couldn't just fire Hank without finding him and confronting him in person and to see that he was returned to the USA.

All of these latest trip expenses would be charged to his pension fund and she needed Hank to sign a paper agreeing to allow the government to set aside these charges from his pension fund.

Ron told her to contact the CIA field office in Istanbul and have them locate Hank and to contact one of the people in Human Resources to handle all of the paperwork for Hank's termination.

It took CIA agents in Istanbul over three weeks to find where Hank Sollenberger was and it wasn't exactly in Istanbul, Hank was on a ship called the Discovery II somewhere in the Black Sea searching for a sunken ship called the Panama Star, somewhere between Istanbul and Odessa.

No one had had any contact with the Discovery II, since she left over three weeks ago.

Beverly advised CIA agents in Istanbul to continue to try to find or make contact with the Discovery II and she would be enroute to meet with Hank Sollenberger.

If they found him they were to detain Hank in Istanbul until she could meet with him. Then she had the CIA Travel Office book her a ticket on the next flight out for Istanbul.

Two days later Beverly arrived in Istanbul, on her arrival the local agents had no additional information on Hank or Discovery II.

They had previously found Hank had spent one night in the Istanbul Hilton. She checked in at the same hotel. Yes, the staff remembered this strange acting American who checked out of the hotel in the middle of the night, saying he was going on an ocean voyage.

They found it very strange, since cruise ships wouldn't be leaving at such an early hour.

They finally got a break because the CIA in Langley was able to contact Luke Turner's wife in Iowa City, who had been on a fishing trip with her father in Northern Canada for the past two weeks, she gave them a GPS coordinate for the Discovery II.

She told them her husband was on some kind of secret mission for the American Government and couldn't say more until he returned home.

They thanked her for her help and told her they were concerned about one of their agents, because he hadn't checked in for several weeks and he was reported to have been with her husband on the Discovery II.

She confirmed there was an agent with her husband.

CIA at Langley contacted Beverly Jenkins in Istanbul and gave her the GPS information given to them from the wife of the Director of Operations for the Discovery ll, who had talked with her husband two nights ago.

Beverly contacted an Air Force Base in Southern Turkey and told them she needed a helicopter for a CIA mission.

After receiving authority for the mission from the Pentagon, they advised Beverly they would pick her up at the Istanbul International Airport at eight o'clock in the morning at the private aircraft operations center.

By eight o'clock the helicopter crew, Beverly and two other CIA agents were enroute to the GPS location of the Discovery II and Hank Sollenberger.

The pilot told Beverly it would take them sometime before they arrived at this GPS location. She could hardly wait.

The mini sub was lowered in the water as Hank was waiting in the operation room to see if they would have any luck finding the grave of the Panama Star.

This time the mini sub slowly made its way down to the ocean floor the sub was approaching the aft of the ship they found.

When the sub got closer to the ship, Luke maneuvered the sub slowly up the aft section of the ship.

Luke screamed, "We've got her, look at that name on the ship!"

Hank could read the words he had been hoping to see, Panama Star; Panama City, Panama. Thank god.

Hank asked, "What else can you see, can you see why she went down?"

Luke responded, "The aft of the ship looks pretty well intact, I'll move the sub around to the port side of the ship."

Luke slowly moved the sub to the port side of the ship and close to the bow they could see in the murky water a huge hole in the hull.

Luke said, "Well that sure would sink her, it looks to me as she had an explosion of some kind and from the looks I would say the explosion was caused on the outside of the hull."

"You don't think she hit something to make a hole like that do you."

"Maybe a 105MM shell, no I would say she has had explosives set off on the outside of the hull."

Luke brought the sub up to where the main deck of the ship should have been and saw another large hole in the center of the main deck, just behind the pilot house.

Luke told Hank, somebody blew the hell out of this lady, she didn't just sink out here she was damn near blown out of the water.

Then they saw an eerie sight, a body of a sailor went by the sub, the body was being moved by the motion of the sub, then they saw a second body.

Hank asked, "Can you bring up those bodies with the sub so we can see how they died?"

"No, we'll have to send divers down."

"How soon can you do it?"

"It won't take too long to get a couple of my people ready to make the dive."

"Good, I need to know if we can see what killed these people."

Luke asked one of his people to bring the sub up so his divers could use it to help find the bodies.

Luke and Hank went up on deck and Luke told two of his men to get suited up to make a dive to bring up some bodies they saw using the sub.

It took about an hour to get the men ready to make the dive and they were taking a large sling device to put the body in to bring it to the surface.

The divers were now in the water following the sub to the sunken ship. Luke was guiding the divers using the sub.

As the divers were closing in on the bodies Hank and Luke heard a helicopter overhead of the Discovery II and a voice over a loudspeaker advising them they were with the US Air Force and were landing on the helicopter pad on the aft of the Discovery II.

Luke said, "Hank it's a good thing we don't have our chopper aboard or I don't know where your people could sit down on this ship."

Hank said, "Yeah, it's a good thing."

Luke told his associate to keep working the sub and help our divers find those two bodies as Hank and he when up on deck.

As soon as the chopper landed, Beverly was out of it and headed directly to where Hank was standing.

Hank would have been happier to see a terrorist coming at him, then to see Beverly Jenkins coming at him with fire coming from both of her eyes.

When she arrived where they were standing, she asked, "Are you Luke Turner?"

"Yes ma'am, I'm Luke Turner and you are?"

"I'm Beverly Jenkins with the CIA. I'm Agent Sollenberger supervisory and I'm here to shut down this operation, because Agent Sollenberger doesn't have the authorization for this mission."

"Ms. Jenkins we have just found the remains of the Panama Star."

"I don't really care. I want this operation shut down right now."

"Yes ma'am, who's going to pay me for all of the time and cost of operating the Discovery II for these past several weeks, and how about the potential danger to America, Agent Sollenberger told me about?"

"Mr. Turner, Agent Sollenberger sees a lot of potential danger for America behind everything that happens around the world."

Just at that moment the two divers came up with one of the bodies they recovered from the Panama Star. Other crew members of the Discovery II were bringing the body on deck.

Hank ran to inspect the body and saw most of the sailor's face was gone. Hank turned the body over and found the sailor had been shot near the top of his head.

Hank said, "Beverly look at this body, this man was executed by being shot in the head and the exit of the bullet has almost blown his face off."

Luke joined in saying, "Yes, and someone has blown a huge hole in the port side of the hull and the main deck, this ship was blown up by somebody and we have film of those holes in the ship."

Beverly was taken aback by the turn of events. She wasn't sure what she should do or say now.

Luke told her his divers were going back down to bring up another body. When they returned with the next body.

Hank found he had been killed the same way.

Beverly told Luke, can you please see how many bodies you can find and bring them up for us.

Luke said, "You mean you want us to continue with our operation?"

"Yes sir."

"Over the next two days the divers recovered nine more bodies all of the people had been killed exactly the same way. They didn't find the bodies of any of the passengers, or the captain.

After the last body had been inspected Beverly said, "Hank it looks like there maybe something to your theory after all."

6

Chance woke, when Juanita came into the tent to bring him to the trailer for breakfast, he couldn't understand anything she was sayings, but he liked the sound of her voice and he understood her motioning.

He got up from his cot and put on his socks, which had dried over night and his shoes which were still very wet.

Chance followed Juanita into the trailer, where Michael's family was just finishing breakfast.

Michael invited him to sit down at the table. Chance was given a plate of cheese, bread and butter. He ate the food hungrily, thinking to himself he was lucky to be alive to be eating breakfast this morning.

Michael told him some of the men from the family left, early this morning to see if they could find out anything about his friends.

Michael said, "Us Gypsies hear many things, because most people think we are only Gypsies and are only interested in what we can steal, but we listen very well.

"Our family makes a little money playing music, some of our women tell fortunes like Juanita; she has the gift.

"If you like I'll have her tell you, your fortune after you have your breakfast."

Chance told Michael that should be very interesting.

When Chance finished eating, Michael asked Juanita to read Chance's fortune, she agreed to do it and took Chance's hand in hers and begin speaking as Michael translated, she said:

"You will live a long life, but right now you are in much danger; but you will live. You will find a beautiful woman to marry very soon and you will have six children; you will not return to your old job, you will find something better to do for you and the world; you will be betrayed by someone close to you; you will find the friends you are seeking; but things will not be as they seem; you will be the way to their freedom.

"I would like to be the woman you love, but it is not to be, you will find someone else. You will know when you meet this woman, she is your love; you will want her more than life itself; that's all I can see of your future."

Chance thought what she said was a lot, he didn't believe in fortune tellers, but she certainly had a lot to say, that was very intriguing.

Two men enter Michael's trailer after they returned from Braila with news. Another Gypsy family told them they saw the bus with the men in uniform yesterday morning and they had two young women in the bus with them, as well as some men without uniforms.

They said the bus was taking these people to a resort called Mountain Top Lodge.

Michael told Chance what the men told him.

Chance asked, "Do you know where this Mountain Top Lodge is?"

"Yes, we know where it is located."

"How far away from us is this lodge?"

"Maybe sixty kilometers, it's on the other side of Braila."

"Can you take me there?"

"First, we must ask the Kris, to seek his counseling."

"Please do it right away. I can pay you for your help."

"My friend with what, will you pay?"

For the first time Chance realized he didn't have his billfold, he had no money; no identification; he had nothing; only the clothes he was wearing and they weren't his.

Chance said, "I'm sorry you're right. I don't have any money. I must have lost my billfold."

Michael said "It's OK we'll see what the Kris says about helping you find your friends."

"Thank you."

Michael, Chance and Juanita made their way to the center of the campground where the Kris was settling a disagreement between family members over some property they borrowed a couple of weeks ago in Bucharest.

They were ordered to divide the property equally, no he said on second thought he would divide the property for them.

The Kris divided the property up between the two family members as Michael was explaining what was going on to Chance.

Michael began speaking on behalf of Chance about helping him rescue his friends being held captive at Mountain Top Lodge.

The Kris listened quietly and with much thought about the consequences to his people.

After a few minutes of talking to some of his closest advisors, the decision was they would take Chance to the area of Mountain Top Lodge, but he wouldn't get any help from the family to try to save his friends from their kidnappers.

Chance could really understand the Kris' feelings about risking the lives of his family to save people they didn't even know.

Chance asked Michael to please thank the Kris for his and his families help. Michael translated Chance's words.

The Kris came to Chance and said in English, "I'm sorry we can't do more to help you."

As Chance was getting into Michael's vehicle, Juanita brought his clothing she had washed for him last night and gave them to him, she kissed him and Michael told him she said she could have loved him, but it was not to be.

She turned away from him as tears were running down her cheeks.

No words were said between Michael and Chance for a long time on the drive toward Braila, both where deep in thought, finally Michael said, "My sister was really taken by you."

"I know, I felt something for her as well, but we are from two different worlds and it would be very hard for either of us to make it in the other ones world."

"My friend, you may know a lot about many things, but you know little about love. Love finds its own world."

"Michael, you're right I know about science, but little about love and life."

Arriving in Braila, Chance saw it was a small village on the Danube River and just as they were leaving town a police vehicle begin following them.

Michael sped up and the police vehicle did the same, Michael began driving faster and the police vehicle was staying close behind him.

They were now traveling at a high rate of speed for the road they were on. They were coming up behind a slow moving car and Michael started to go around it when he saw a truck coming around the curve heading straight for them, he swung his vehicle back behind the slow moving car and as soon as the truck past them, he was back out trying to get around the car that was impeding his progress.

Just as he pulled back into his traffic lane in front of the car he had past; the police vehicle started coming around the car as another truck was coming down the mountain directly at the police vehicle.

The police vehicle had no choice, but to pull back in behind the slow moving car to avoid hitting the truck head on.

Michael told Chance we are coming to a big curve in a few minutes and when we do. I'm going to slow down and you jump out, because I don't know if the police are after me or you.

If it me they want, maybe I spend a couple of nights in jail again, if it's you they are looking for, who knows what will happen to you.

The Mountain Top Lodge is somewhere ahead of us. I'm not sure how far it is. As he said that they were in the curve, Michael slowed down and told Chance to open the door and jump.

Chance opened the door and although Michael had slowed down he was still going at a fairly high speed as Chance rolled himself out the door of the vehicle.

He hit the soft ground of the shoulder of the road and rolled down into a ditch and kept rolling until he hit a small tree; he grabbed hold of it to stop him.

Chance lay quietly and tried to decide if he was all right. He moved his arms and legs both of them seemed to be OK, his face and arms were covered with scraps and scratches, but other than that he was all right.

Chance crawled back up where he could see the roadway and in the distance he saw the car they and the police vehicle had been behind it was now about a quarter of a mile away from him.

Seeing the car's location he had to believe Michael and the police vehicle had to be long gone away from him.

He looked around him and saw he was in a large forest on a hillside, which looked to Chance like the foothills of the Rocky Mountains.

He decided he needed to get away from the edge of the road, but keep it in sight of it to use it to help guide him to Mountain Top Lodge.

Chance got up off of his knees and started walking up the hill or mountain, whichever it was and tried to stay in sight of the road.

He saw his borrowed pants and shirt had not fared well with his jump from the vehicle, they were torn and dirty and the palms of his hands were bleeding, he hadn't noticed them bleeding before.

What a road racing trip he was having, yes he wanted a little adventure in his life, but this was not the adventure he was looking for.

Yesterday he had been kidnapped; almost drowned; paddled for hours and hours and for who knew how far on a piece of a shipping crate; dodged uniformed men searching for him; and captured by Gypsies.

Then there was today, he had been chased by police; jumped out of a moving vehicle; was now hiding from police and was in a Romanian Forest looking for a place called Mountain Top Lodge and when he found it or if he found it, what could he do to free his companions?

First things first, he had to find Mountain Top Lodge, before he could work out a way to free his friends.

He kept walking and the walking it was getting harder as the climb was getting steeper. He had to rest for a few minutes if he dared, he could use some water to drink.

Suddenly he felt like he had a fever, his head was pounding from getting hit with the pistol yesterday, he forgot that when he was listing his troubles awhile ago.

He could remember it now, with his head pounding like it was. He had no choice he had to keep walking. He could hear a noise ahead of him, it sounded like water running.

He was sure it was water, he pressed on until he came upon a beautiful clear mountain stream flowing down the mountain. His first thought is this water OK to drink, it didn't matter he had to quench his thirst.

He slowly dropped to his knees, god his knees hurt.

He got down on his elbows, god did his elbows hurt. Chance didn't have anything on his body that didn't hurt. It was only a question of what hurt worse at that moment.

Chance took a small drink of the mountain water and it tasted good, then he drink a lot of water. After drinking as much as he could, he took off his clothes and began trying to wash the blood off of his knees; elbows; hands and a hundred other places on his body.

He took one of his socks and wet it in the cold water and put the wet sock on the back of his head to ease the pain. The sun was shining through the trees and the warmth felt good on all of his aching body parts.

Chance lay down completely naked on some grass near the stream to rest after he had washed all of his clothes and laid them out to dry. He wished the grass was softer and the sun a little hotter on him.

His head felt better and he fell asleep for a few minutes.

He woke up to find a beautiful blonde woman stand at his feet staring at his naked body.

Chance tried to cover himself up with his hands, but the woman said in English, "You're a little too late, I've already seen all you've got, oh well. I'm sure you don't understand what I said anyway."

Chance found his clothes and put them on and said, "I'm sorry if I frighten you."

"Oh, you didn't frighten me. I was enjoying the view and you speak English."

"Yes, I speak American English. I'm an American. My name is Chance Taylor."

"Hi, I'm Shannon O'Hara from Ireland, what are you doing here, besides laying out here without any clothes on?"

"I'm looking for my friends who are supposed to be at a place called Mountain Top Lodge, do you know where it is?"

"Yes, I think I do, I saw a sign for it about ten miles up the mountain."

"What's an Irish Lass doing in the mountains of Romanian?"

"I'm here on summer holiday, hiking from Odessa to Bucharest."

Before Chance responded, he took time to really look at this adventurous woman; she was about five foot six, with the biggest bright blue eyes he had ever seen and her hair was as golden blonde as a Kansas wheat field in June.

"That's a long hike, are you traveling by yourself?"

"Now I am, my friend decided to take a train when we arrived in Galati yesterday, she couldn't walk another step she said and begged me to go with her, but I told her no.

"I set a goal of hiking from Odessa to Bucharest and I intended to finish the trip, even if I had to it alone."

"Good for you, where's your hiking gear?"

"I left it lying near the road and followed this brook and to find a place to pee, but found you instead."

"Don't let me stop you."

"OK, I won't."

She went behind some thick bushes to relieve herself and soon came back where Chance was at.

Shannon said, "Whew, I feel better. You don't have any gear with you?"

"No, it's a long story."

"It's getting late, why don't you let me get my gear and you can help me set up camp here for the night and you can tell me your long story?"

"I don't know. I think I better push on to try to find my friends."

"Bad idea, the climb gets much harder from here on and walking along the road you're likely to get hit by a car or a lorry.

"Walking in the woods you may wind up in some ravine, there some rough country ahead."

"You make staying here for the night sound very inviting, instead of where I might end up if I try going on. Ending up in the bottom of a ravine would not help my friends very much would it?"

"It's settled. I'll get my gear and you can help me carry it."

Shannon and Chance walked back to the roadway and gathered up her things and came back to the same location where Chance had been resting.

She beginning taking things out of her backpack; she had a small tent she sit up and some cooking utensils; food of various kinds and a sleeping bag.

Chance was surprised of what all she had in her backpack and wondered how she could carry it all.

She told him she was a flight attendant for British Airways and lived and worked out of London.

She had a month off and was doing her normal summer thing hiking across Europe. She had been doing it since she was sixteen.

She was born and raised in, of course Shannon, Ireland and she was named for the City.

Her parents still lived there and after she finished her degree at Trinity College or as some people called it now the University of Dublin, but she said she preferred the old name.

She had a degree in Electronic Engineering, but became a flight attendant to travel the world while she was young and unmarried.

Chance told her all about what had happened to him over the past two days, but he didn't go into details about his line of work.

He did tell her he had gone to the University of Chicago and lived in Albuquerque, New Mexico.

She had been to Chicago many times, but never to New Mexico.

She prepared them something to eat from her variety of prepackaged foods; Chance ate it, but thought he would have preferred a nice steak dinner with a salad and a baked potato and a glass of wine.

After hours of conversation, Shannon told him he could get in the tent with her and she would unzip her sleeping bag to allow him somewhere to sleep. She said it would be very close quarters in the tent, but it would be better then sleeping on the ground with nothing to lie on or to cover up with.

As Chance lay next to Shannon, he thought back to Juanita's fortune telling this morning and wondered if Shannon could be the one he was to fall in love with.

Before going to sleep, Shannon told him she was going to go with him to help him rescue his friends.

7

everly Jenkins told Hank he could stay in Istanbul and work with the CIA agents to see what they could find out about the missing doctors and their companions.

She was returning to Langley at once to talk with Ron Parsons about what they found on the sunken Panama Star and the possibility Hank's theory regarding the break-in in Russia and the missing scientists had validity to it.

No sooner had Beverly left Istanbul then Hank started pushing the Istanbul CIA Chief, Richard Queen to let him take a couple of agents and pose as tourists in Romania to see if they could get a lead on Drs. Taylor and Brown.

As usual, Hank was relentless, when he had his mind set on doing something, so just to get Hank out of his hair, Richard Queen agreed.

Chief Queen assigned CIA Agents Tom Parker and Rick Byrd to set-up a trip to Romania and take Hank Sollenberger with them pretending to be tourist.

Hank had studied the location where the Panama Star was sunk and the coastline of Romania and he thought the kidnappers probably came ashore somewhere near the town of Jurilovca.

Tom was the agent in charge of the investigation and he decided they would go by ferry from Istanbul to Varna, Bulgaria from there they would rent a van and drive to Romania.

Tom Parker was a retired bird Colonel from the Army Special Forces who had spent years working with the CIA and when he retired after his twenty-years of service, he just moved from the Army to the CIA.

Tom was a West Point graduate and an experienced decorated combat veteran seeing service in Vietnam and every combat operation America was involved in after that; some well knowing to the public; some that were not known by the public at all.

Rick Byrd was a career CIA Agent who specialist in languages and had trained with Colonel Parker with his Special Forces Unit in the Gulf War.

Together they formed a good team, but would have never been prepared to work with Hank Sollenberger.

Tom arranged for camping gear to take with them and planned to pick up food and other provisions in Varna.

He had British Passports made for each of them and purchased English made casual clothes for the three of them to take on the trip to look like typical British Tourists.

After making all of these arrangements, they were ready to leave Istanbul to Varna in the morning.

Hank was excited and anxious, since he had never been allowed to go on a real CIA operation. Hereto-for, he only went on then in his mind.

Tom Parker and Rick Byrd were real pros and had been with the CIA for several years, with an excellent reputation for achieving results.

Chief Queen told Tom privately to watch out for Hank on this mission, because he had a questionable reputation at CIA Headquarters; a bit of a screw-up.

The ferry boat trip was uneventful and on arrival in Varna they passed through formal procedures without any problems and picked-up the rental van Tom booked from Istanbul.

From Varna they drove up the coast to Constanta, Romania, spent the night in a small hotel,

Hank was filled with anticipation of what tomorrow would bring. He was sure they would find a clue as to where his two scientists were at when they got to Jurilovca.

Hank could hardly sleep, he was up and down all night long and when it was time to get up he had finally fallen asleep, when his telephone wake-up call came.

He dressed as quickly as he could and met Tom and Rick in the breakfast room of the hotel.

Tom said unless you're a good cook you better enjoy your breakfast, because Rick is a lousy cook.

Hank never gave much thought about food; sometimes he would get busy thinking about some plot or theory and forget to eat and would go all day without anything but coffee.

However, with the dire warning he had about Rick's cooking, he sat down and ate a hearty breakfast. Then they were back in the van and traveling toward Jurilovca.

Arriving in Jurilovca, they spent time around the waterfront, maybe Rick couldn't cook, but he could speak Romanian. He engaged in conversations with several of the men working around the docks.

Rick offered to buy the men drinks after they finished work that day.

They told him they finished work around six and said they would meet him and his friends at a bar across from the docks.

Hank couldn't wait to hear what Rick learned from the men about the ship that sunk just off of the coast.

Rick told him the men hadn't even heard about a ship sinking, at least that was the story they were telling so far. Maybe after a few drinks their memories might improve.

They drove around the town, which didn't take long, since it wasn't a very big town, they found a campsite and Tom and Rick went about setting up their camp for the night.

Hank's only help came in the form of carrying some of the camping gear from the van and he couldn't do that very well.

Hank had never been camping and watching his associate's set-up a tent; unfold cots; and seeing ice coolers and camping stove was as strange to him as if Hank had been watching spacemen from some other galaxy unload their spaceship and set up gear.

After the campsite was completed, it was time to go back to the bar to meet the dock workers.

Hank, told Tom and Rick, maybe I should stay here and guard our things.

Tom said, "That's probably a good idea to have someone here to look after the camping equipment.

"As they drove off leaving Hank at the camp, Tom told Rick, I don't think Hank was up to sitting in a bar half of the night, drinking with dock workers and fishermen.

He also said, "I'm pretty sure he wouldn't be a great guard if someone wanted to take our stuff either."

Rick laughed and said, "Hell, he wouldn't be worth a damn, even helping the crooks load the stuff up."

Tom and Rick laughed at the thought of how Hank would react if someone actually came to the campsite trying to steal something.

Tom was a little bit off with his guess of half of the night as to how long they would be buying drinks at the bar, it was all night.

By the time they got in the van to drive back to their campsite they could see the sun breaking through an early morning fog over the bay.

What a night, they didn't think there were as many people in the whole town as they were buying drinks for and just what did they learn for their efforts, a big fat nothing!

By the time they arrived at their campsite they needed to go to bed, but Hank was waiting to hear what they learned after being gone all night.

Tom spoke first and said, "Don't even ask."

Tom and Rick went directly into their tent and on their cots and went to sleep.

Dr. al-Sadr told Charles Brown we will soon be getting the equipment and materials you will need for you to begin your work.

"I expect my good friend, Colonel Zaro Zmitrovitch and your new assistant Dr. Boris Zortman should be arriving here in a few days, but until then relax and enjoy yourself."

Dr. al-Sadr then said, "You may be interested to see the truck coming here this afternoon, my friends have brought it special delivery all the way from Southern Iran, it's a very valuable cargo, you and your friends will enjoy seeing this cargo, the kind of cargo men's dreams are made of."

Then he laughed as he had just told him a very funny joke.

Later that afternoon a large canvas covered truck pulled up to the front of the lodge and Charles could see several men with automatic weapons getting out the truck and al-Sadr greeting the men.

After a few minutes of conversation, the men from the truck began unloading boxes from the truck. Several boxes were unloaded from the rear of the truck and sit aside at the back of the truck, then the men began unloading different looking boxes, these were metal boxes.

These boxes, they sit on the porch of the lodge and al-Sadr opened each of the boxes as they were brought to the porch.

After several of the boxes had being opened and inspected by al-Sadr he called Charles Brown to bring the others out to see what his friends had brought him.

All of the captives came out on the porch and al-Sadr said, "Close your eyes and come over to this side of the porch and when I say look, everyone open their eyes."

The captives did as they were told and when they all had been guided by their guards to where al-Sadr was located he said, "OK, you can open your eyes!"

The captives opened their eyes and saw box after box of gold bars.

Al-Sadr said, "Have you ever seen anything as beautiful as this?"

Charles said, "No, it is beautiful."

"Yes my little friends, when my men finish unloading the truck we will have one hundred million dollars worth of this beautiful stuff, a gift from our friends in Iraq who stole it from Kuwait, so we stole it from them."

Al-Sadr continued, "Now I am ready to take delivery of the material for Dr. Brown's project he's doing for me."

Two days later, four large trucks pulled up in front of the lodge and al-Sadr went out to meet his guests.

Al-Sadr hugged a man who got out of the first truck, then the two men went back to the second truck in the convey where Brown saw al-Sadr introduced by the man from the first truck to a man who arrived in the second truck.

The three men came into the lodge and al-Sadr introduced Brown to the two men; the man in the first truck was, Colonel Zaro Zmitrovitch and the second man was, Dr. Boris Zortman.

Zortman said, "How do you do Dr. Brown. I am very pleased to meet you. I've heard so many good things about you."

"I sorry Dr. Zortman, I haven't heard anything about you."

"Well, perhaps Russian intelligence is better than the Americans. I know of your work at Sandia and I will be honored to be working with you on this project."

"Dr. Zortman, you have experience in the same field as I do?"

"Yes, until three days ago. I was the Director of a Nuclear Weapons Research Center in Russia."

"Why did you quit?"

"I found a job paying me a lot of money, that's why I'm here."

Al-Sadr broke in and said, "Dr. Brown, Dr. Zortman will be assisting you with the work you will be doing for me and during you and your friends stay here.

"Colonel Zmitrovitch will be taking over the security of the lodge.

"He was previously with Russian Intelligence and before that, he was a member of the KGB, so security will be in good hands during your stay."

The captives thought there was already was enough security around the lodge that they couldn't see any way out.

Al-Sadr told Brown and Zortman to come with him he wanted to show them where they would be working.

They followed him out of the lodge and down a small path leading behind the lodge and after walking through an area with numerous trees and brush they came to a large metal building.

Al-Sadr opened the door and they could see there was nothing inside the building; the building had concrete floors and plenty of overhead lights, but nothing else.

Brown asked if the building was new, because the concrete looked like it had been recently poured.

He was told; "Yes it was. We built it especially for you and Dr. Taylor to do your work in."

Brown asked, "Where is the equipment and materials we need to do this work for you?"

"Don't worry it's in the four trucks that just arrived courtesy of Colonel Zmitrovitch and the Russian Government, the Russians don't know they're supplying all of it to us.

"Tomorrow at this time the lab will be completely set-up and be ready for you to begin building my bombs."

Chance woke up and sat straight up and hit his head of the top of the small tent he had been sleeping in with Shannon.

Hitting the tent didn't hurt his head, but where he had been hit in the back of his head with the pistol two days ago sure did.

Chance looked over where Shannon had been sleeping and saw she was already out of the tent. He extracted himself out of the tent and saw Shannon busy washing herself in the small stream.

She turned and saw Chance and said "Good morning, how did you sleep?

Chance told her he must have done very well since he hardly remembered lying down last night.

Shannon had made tea and asked if he would like some, indeed he would and he said if you had about two hundred aspirins. I could use those too.

Shannon didn't have two hundred aspirins, but she did have some in her backpack if she could find them.

After spending a few minutes looking, she handed Chance four aspirins, he down them with a glass of mountain stream water.

Now he was ready for tea, but a good cup of hot American coffee would have been better Chance thought.

However, the tea did taste pretty good.

They had a breakfast of hard bread; cheese and an orange. After they finished their meal, Shannon began packing up her things in her backpack and took down her tent and carefully folded it up to fit in her backpack.

She rolled up her sleeping bag and tied it neatly under her backpack. She was ready to help Chance find his friends.

She picked up the backpack and placed her arms through the straps and told Chance let's go.

Chance and Shannon began walking up the mountain, before too long they came to one of those ravines Shannon warned Chance about last night, they had to go up to the roadway to get around it.

Chance said, "Wow, I'm glad I followed your advice about not trying to climbing this mountain last night in the dark, or as you told me. I would probably be at the bottom of this ravine now.

"Always listen to what I tell you and you'll make it all right."

"Thanks, I'll listen to you."

They continued climbing up the mountain and when they got to the top. Chance thought Mountain Top Lodge must be getting very close and said so to Shannon.

"Sorry, the lane I saw the sign for Mountain Top Lodge was on the mountain ahead of us."

"Oh thanks, that's just what I wanted to hear."

"Oh, I knew you would, look at this way while we are going downhill at least we won't being going down nearly as much as where we started from this morning. So it will be a much easier climb to the top of the next mountain."

"Well, that will certainly help, Shannon why don't you let me carry your backpack now. I feel funny letting you do all of the work."

"You must be one of those modern thinking men, don't you know it's the woman place to do the work while you men watch!"

"Give me the backpack!"

"OK, on one condition tell me you head not hurting."

"OK, my head is not hurting."

"Now, I don't know whether to believe you or not."

Shannon took off her backpack and gave it to Chance, as Chance began carry it downhill he felt like it might push him on down the hill and wondered how this young woman could possible carry this thing all the way from Odessa.

That was the first time Chance got the point about women being the stronger sex, for God sake they had the babies didn't they.

Chance continued carrying the backpack not only down the mountain, but back up the next mountain, he couldn't let a hundred-twenty pound woman out do him.

He made it down all right, but as he was climbing the next mountain, he dragged farther and farther behind Shannon, who had not realized she was walking off and leaving him.

She stopped and looked around and saw Chance must have been a quarter of a mile behind her. She started to go back to help him, but Chance yelled to her just wait for me.

Chance kept climbing the mountain, one painful step after the next painful step until he was about a hundred feet from Shannon and he fell down on one knee.

Shannon raced to him and grabbed the backpack and kept him from falling backwards.

Chance said, "Sorry."

"It's all right you're not use to carrying backpacks across Europe."

"I didn't know I was in this bad of shape." "No one ever does until they try to do something they never done before."

Shannon put on the backpack and helped Chance regain his upright position and they pushed on up the mountain.

When they made it almost to the top Shannon said, "There's the sign I saw yesterday for Mountain Top Lodge."

A few more steps and they saw the lane leading off of the highway to Mountain Top Lodge, they turned onto the lane and began walking toward the lodge, they didn't get very far until they came to a gate blocking the lane with a sign saying in several different languages "Closed Keep Out".

Chance and Shannon went around the gate and continued walking up the lane until a man with an automatic weapon came out of the woods and motioned for them to stop.

Shannon started speaking to him in English. He held his finger up to his mouth to tell her to stop talking and motioned for them to leave.

Chance took hold of Shannon's arm and turned her around to go back toward the highway, they started walking back down the lane when another guard appeared.

It was the one who had hit Chance with his pistol. He shouted to Chance to stop where he was.

Chance did and turned around and recognized the guard from the ship. Then both of the guards took hold of Chance arms and threw him to the ground and then grabbed Shannon and forced her to her knees.

One of the men called on his radio to the lodge and a few minutes later a vehicle arrived and Chance and Shannon were roughly put into the vehicle and the driver turned the vehicle around and drove them to the lodge.

When they arrived there the guards took them out of the vehicle and marched them inside the lodge. Arriving in the lodge they were careful greeted by Chance's friends.

A few minutes past before an important looking and acting man came into the living room of the lodge and said, "Dr. Chance Taylor, how kind of you to join us here at Mountain Top Lodge and you brought a very lovely young woman with you, doubly kind of you."

"I had no choice, you have my friends."

"Oh, you had a choice, but you made the wrong one."

"We'll see about that."

"Let me introduce myself, I'm Dr. al-Sadr. I'm your host while you are here and as I explained to your friends when they arrived, if you try to escape you will be killed; if you don't perform the work I want you to, one by one your friends will be killed.

"I will tell you, you wouldn't enjoy watching them die, have you ever seen anyone skinned alive; oh it's an ugly sight, it makes my stomach turn just to think about it.

"You do as I tell you and you will be treated well, you don't and you will hate the treatment you will receive. Do we understand each other; good?"

"I will show you to your rooms, Dr. Taylor your room has been waiting for you, but we'll have to make up a room for Miss, what's your name?"

"Shannon O'Hara."

"Like Scarlet O'Hara from Gone with the Wind, are you? I hope not, she was a pain in the butt and a schemer."

Al-Sadr showed Chance to his room and Chance was surprised to find clothing in his size wanting for him in his room.

Next, al-Sadr took Shannon to a room and asked if she had brought any clothing with her in her backpack that he saw that was brought in with her.

She told him she had her own clothing. He told her as soon as his people went through her backpack to see that she didn't have any weapons. He would have it brought to her.

Al-Sadr came back to Chance's room and knock on the door, Chance opened the door and al-Sadr came into his room and said, "Dr. Taylor you can't begin to know how much I appreciate you come here to me.

"I don't know how you survived drowning in the sea, but I'm glad you did, because Dr. Brown is going to need your help building a few bombs for me and you're the one who knows the best way to make the triggers for them.

"Dr. Brown is going to be really happy to have you here. You know you can go talk with your friends anytime you like;

you have the freedom of the camp as long as you don't try to escape.

"All right Dr. al-Sadr. I'll keep that in mind."

Al-Sadr turned around and left the room. Chance soon left his room and returned to the living room where all of his friends were gathered, they begin hugging him and telling him they were sure he drowned when he fell into the sea.

He told them he almost did.

Charles said, "Chance, when you fell in the water and I saw you go under my heart sank with you."

He put his arms around Chance and hugged him as hard as he could.

"I still can't believe your alive, how did you keep from drowning and how did you ever find us?"

"It's a long story better told some other time."

Shannon came in the room and Chance introduced her to everyone; Dr. Charles Brown, Anmend Soekarmo and his sister, Kerida; Curtis La Salle and PJ Murphy and Annie Taylor.

After he introduced her to everyone he explained who each one of them was and how come they came to be with him on the trip and told the others how he met Shannon and who she was and how she had helped him find the lodge.

He only deleted the part of the story about being naked when they met.

Chance asked, "Has anyone figured out how to get out of this place yet?"

Charles replied, "They have guards and TV cameras everywhere, so I think we better do what they tell us and if we do they would let us go."

"Charles do you believe them, who are they, do you know that?"

"Al-Sadr is some kind of an al-Qaeda leader and he's got a Russian Colonel and a Russian Nuclear Scientist helping him; plus his al-Qaeda men and Russian's ex KGB people. They're not people you mess with."

"Charlie, I'll tell you something if we don't get out of here the bombs we're going to make are going to kill thousands and thousands of Americans, we got to find a way out, do you really think al-Sadr is not going to kill us when we finish making these bombs, if you do you're dreaming. He's never going to lets us go."

Later that night after everyone was in bed, Chance opened his bedroom window, climbed out of it and carefully avoided getting into the light and slowly crawled on his hands and knees until he was safely away from the house and into the woods.

He worked his way to the lane they came down to the lodge on and stayed hidden in the woods alongside the lane. He got to the gate at the lanes entrance, where he and Shannon were captured by the guards.

Chance couldn't believe how easy it had been for him to get out of the camp.

He was now entering the highway and saw a truck coming down the road and Chance stood out in the road and waved it down.

The truck stopped just before it hit him, a man opened the door of the truck and said, "Dr. Taylor you didn't understand what I told you this afternoon did you?"

Chance started to run back into the woods when two of al-Sadr's men grabbed him by his arms and pulled him back into the truck.

When they arrived back at the lodge, al-Sadr had all of the hostages brought to the living room where Chance was now bound with plastic straps around his wrist with his arms behind his back lying in a prone position on the floor.

Al-Sadr said, "Dr. Taylor, I'm going to show you what happens when you disobey me."

Chance's head was on the floor being held down with a very large foot on it and Chance heard a loud gunshot and PJ Murphy fell on the floor next to where Chance was lying. PJ's had almost all of the back of his head blown off.

Blood was pouring from his head and running on the floor onto Chance's face. After Chance had been held on the floor for several minutes, he was picked up off of the floor by two guards.

Chance's face was covered with PJ's blood.

Chance could hear his friends crying and screaming with fear and Curtis screaming at him that he killed his friend, my love.

Chance wasn't able to see his friends with his head held down by a guard and PJ's blood clouding his vision.

Chance was dragged down stairs and taken to a dark room and thrown onto a concrete floor with the plastic straps still on his wrists with his arms behind his back.

Before the guards left, one of them leaned down and said you don't learn very well do you and then hit him in the back of the head knocking him unconscious.

The guards shut and locked the door of Chance's cell.

8

After almost three weeks in Romania Hank, Tom and Rick had found out nothing about either the sunken ship or any of the missing people.

The one thing that had happened by this time, Hank had learned to speak Romanian, since it had its roots in Latin, the same as French; Italian; Spanish and Portuguese, which Hank could already speak; he could now speak Romanian as well as Rick, maybe better.

They had traveled as far north as Tulcea and back south all the way back to Constanta; from Constanta they went west to Slobozia and Hank felt any farer in that direction and they would be getting too close to Bucharest, he was sure the kidnappers wouldn't take a chance with seven American hostages being in such a large city.

No, Hank thought they would be closer to the coast, either in a small town or a secluded farm location.

Tom suggested they drive north on Romanian Highway Route 21 to Galati and work their way back to the coast from there.

Hank and Rick agreed, because they sure weren't getting anywhere in any of the places they had been so far.

Tom told Hank, "Field work is boring; we spend hours; days; weeks; months and sometime years searching for information, you have to learn the four "P's" to be a field agent: perseverance; persistence; perspiration and patience."

Hank had little patience; or perspiration, however he was excellent at persisting and persevering to the point of exasperating everyone he worked with.

Tom and Rick hadn't decided whether to kill Hank or their boss, Chief Queen for sticking Hank with them.

So far, they had managed to keep their cool. How much longer it would last, who knew?

Hank either talked excessively or not at all, sometimes speaking in different languages in one sentence. Hank was obviously brilliant, but a complete nut!

Arriving in Galati, they sit up their camp site just outside of the city. Hank still was useless helping them with the work.

Tom finally told him to please just stay out of the way. After they finished setting up camp, the three of them when back into town.

Tom and Rick went to the nearest bar to start conversations with the locals to see if they could gleam any information about the missing scientists and their friends.

Hank went around to various stores talking to the storekeepers and their customers to see if they had seen any Americans in town recently, he told the people he spoke with he was to meet some of his friends here last week, but he couldn't get here until today.

No, no one had seen or talked to any Americans here for a long time.

They spend four days in Galati without any clues or information about their people, the decision was made to go to Braila tomorrow.

Hank couldn't believe seven Americans could just disappear in Romania without any one seeing or hearing something about them.

On their way out of town Tom stopped to fill up the van with fuel, Hank got out of the van to walk around a bit before they left town.

A young woman he talked to in one of the stores approached him and asked if he was the man looking for some Americans. He told her he was.

Hank was sure he was about to get a lead on their scientists. The woman said, a few weeks ago two young women, British she thought, but maybe Americans came through town carrying backpacks, one of them stayed in the store for awhile waiting for a bus or train and the other one went on hiking by herself to Bucharest.

Hank's disappointment was showed on his face, but he thanked her for telling him about the women.

The woman said, "I sorry if it was not your friends."

Before they got into Braila they found a campsite and Tom and Rick went through the normal ritual of sitting up camp.

Hank told them he was going to walk to town to see who he could talk with.

Walking along the road he was passed by several vehicles before he got to town, one of the trucks that passed him stopped at a roadside vegetable stand.

He watched as the two men in the truck purchased almost all of the produce the stand had and then watched them load their purchases into the truck.

As Hank past by the truck he heard the men speaking in Russian, but gave little thought to, it since Russia had been in control of Romania for many years and they were very close to the old USSR border.

Hank continued walking until he came to an intersection of Highway 21 and a smaller road with a sign pointing toward Macin and Constanta, Hank instinctively turned on the small road and kept walking until he was at the edge of town.

Here he saw a Gypsy Fortune Teller sitting outside of a small tent waiting for a customer to tell them their fortunes.

As Hank continued walking passed her, the young woman called out to him and asked if she could read his fortune?

Hank first said no, and then he said OK. Reluctantly he followed her into her small tent and sit down on a folding chair in front of a small table covered with a black cloth with her sitting across from him.

She asked how he would like for her to read his fortune.

Hank replied, "I don't know, how many ways can you, read my fortune?"

"Many ways, using cards, reading your palm."

"What's the difference?"

"Reading your palm is best, but it cost more."

"OK, let's do my fortune reading my palm."

The Fortune Teller started reading his palm: you don't every do any work with your hands, only maybe by using a computer; you are very smart, you work only by using your brain; right now you're searching for something, maybe for someone; you are an American; you will find whatever you are looking for, but it will be hard for you to get it; perhaps what you are looking for is very close to you right now.

She stopped.

Hank asked, "What else do you see?" "To see more you must pay more, OK." "OK, I'll pay more, keep reading." "First, the money!"

Hank took out his money and let her take the amount she was charging him.

Hank put the rest of the money that was left in his pants pocket and then he took out his billfold and handed her an American One Hundred Dollar Bill.

Hank said, "I want a very good fortune, one that tells me where my friends are, seven missing Americans, do you understand, if you help me find them. I'll give you ten more one hundred dollar bills."

"Chance?"

"Do you know Dr. Chance Taylor?"

"I know Chance, my brother and I helped him." "Where is he?"

"I'm not sure, my brother was taking him someplace where we heard his friends where, we don't know if he got to them or not."

"Where was your brother taking him?"

"I don't know for sure, you'll have to ask my brother, Michael?"

"Where is your brother, let's go talk with him."

"Michael is in jail, he was arrested taking Chance to the place we think his friends are at."

"Can we see him at the jail or can we pay to get him out?"

"If you have enough money, we can get him out of jail."

"OK, let's get him out of jail."

Hank told her his name was Hank Sollenberger and asked her name, she told him she was Juanita.

Together they begin walking toward town, arriving in town Hank saw Tom and Rick and told them what Juanita told him about Dr. Chance Taylor.

The four of them went to the jail to get Michael out.

When the four of them went into the jail, Juanita told the jailer she wanted to get her brother out of jail; the jailer told her he doubt if she had enough money to pay him out of jail.

Tom told the jailer perhaps we do, we are Michael's cousins from England. The jailer told them an amount due was equal to about one hundred pounds sterling.

Tom took out his wallet and gave the jailer the money in Romanian currency. Rick told the jailer to write them a receipt for paying the fine.

He took some time finding a receipt book, but finally he wrote the receipt for the payment of the fine and gave the receipt to Rick.

The jailer left them in the office and as he went back to where the cells of the prisoners were located, a few minutes later the jailer and Michael came into the office where Juanita; Hank; Tom and Rick were waiting.

As soon as Juanita saw Michael she rushed up to him and hugged him and said "Our British cousins have paid your fine to get you out of jail, isn't that wonderful."

As soon as Michael's things taken from him when he was put in jail were returned to him the group left the jail.

Michael said, "Who are these men?"

Hank replied, "We're friends of Chance's and we've come here to help him and his friends get safely home, can you help us?"

"I'll help you a little, the last time I tried helping. I was put in jail and I never thought they would let me out."

"Fine, just help us a little bit; tell us where Chance is."

"I could only tell you where he was going to find his friends, we had information his friends were at a place called Mountain Top Lodge. It's about halfway to Galati on the top of the highest mountain between here and Galati."

"Can you show us where it is?"

"No, I'm going home to my wife and kids. I done enough already to endanger my family, follow the highway to Galati and look for the sign for Mountain Top Lodge along the road."

"OK, Michael, thank you for your help."

Juanita said, "Hank, you owe me ten more one hundred dollar bills."

"Yes I do."

Hank took out his billfold and counted out ten one hundred dollar bills; then he thanked her again for her help.

Michael and Juanita got into Michael's truck which had been parked at the police station since he was arrested. After starting the truck they turned on the small road headed to Braila away from Galati.

Hank, Tom and Rick drove in their van in the direction of Galati on the same highway they came over this morning.

Michael was right, they found a sign indicting the turn off for Mountain Top Lodge. Tom turned the vehicle onto the lane, but only a few car lengths off of the highway they came to gate with a sign in various languages stating the lodge was closed.

Tom stopped the van and started to get out when he saw a guard approaching with an automatic weapon.

Rick asked, "Is the lodge closed, we came from England and were told it was a very nice place to stay."

The guard replied, "Sorry, the lodge is closed for remodeling this year, but reopens next year, please come back then."

Rick thanked the man and then asked how come you have to guard the lodge if it's not open and he was told during their remodeling, thieves stole much of the materials being used to remodel the lodge, lots of Gypsies live around here and they steal everything they can get their hands on.

Rick thanked the guard again and Tom turned the van around and left.

Hank asked, "Is that all were going to do? When are we going to see if our missing scientists are in there?"

Tom replied, "Patience, we've got to get a lot more information then we have before we go busting in there, weren't you the one telling us about the size of the hole in the Panama Star and the eleven sailors with the back of their heads blown off.

"Are you ready to have the same thing happen to you?

"These people holding our nuclear scientists and their friends are killers, my guess from looking at the automatic weapon the guard was holding and the tactics they're using; these people are al-Qaeda lead by someone who has spent years planning this project."

"I guess you're right, but how long do you think we will have to wait, before we go in?"

"I doubt you will ever be going in, you don't have the training for this kind of operation and you could get yourself killed or worse get somebody else killed."

9

Tom Parker called CIA Headquarters in Langley, Virginia for the Assistant Director of The CIA, Ron Parsons to tell him what kind of help he needed to rescue the nuclear scientists.

Tom was on hold for a few minutes before Ron picked up his phone and said, "How's my luckiest CIA Agent doing in Romania?"

Hello Ron, well I would say my luck is hold out, we're sure we've located Dr. Chance Taylor and we guess we have found the rest of the folks traveling with him,"

"You mean you don't know for sure that the other missing people are with him?"

"No, but I'm pretty sure there with him. We have reliable information from the folks who helped Dr. Taylor find where his friends were being held and we certainly believe they're all there together."

"Tom, what do you need to get our people out of there?"

"I'll tell you what I need to start with is surveillances on the area, where they're being held. I have the coordinates of the location and what I want to know is how many guards are there and the type of weapons they have?"

"OK Tom, give me the coordinates and I'll see what I can find out for you."

Tom gave him the information on the coordinates of the property.

"Then Tom said, "Ron, from the little I've seen of the enemy and their weapons we're dealing with al-Qaeda."

"Are you sure about it, Tom?"

"I've only see one of the guards and his weapon, but what I observed from him and his automatic weapon, it's my opinion they're al-Qaeda all right."

"What the hell do you think they're up to with two nuclear scientists?"

"Ron, if you want my opinion, they're building bombs like Hank Sollenberger has tried to tell you folks, I believe him.

"I think he is right about material being stolen from Russia and brought here to build nuclear devices to set off in America and it scares the hell of me, so we've better getting them before they get us!

"One more thing Ron, if you ever send Hank, to work with me again, I'm retiring right then, he's a nut.

"So pity me, because I really believe he's called this right from the beginning, even if he does drive me and everybody else crazy!"

"Now Tom, you know you will never retire unless one of the bad guys kills you, because you know you love us and love your job too much."

"Well I love it, but if I ever found a rich widow, I'm out of here!"

"You've been looking for one have you, Tom?"

"You know I haven't, you never let me stay in one place long enough to look if I wanted to find one."

"Don't kid me Tom, I've heard all about how you're still in love with a gal who married somebody else, while you were serving in Nam. She really broke your heart, didn't she?"

"I guess she did, because it's been a long time since Viet Nam."

"OK, I'm sorry I brought it up, what else do you think you're going to need to get our people out of there?"

"Ron, I want a Special Forces Company, who knows what they're doing and can take orders. We're going to need them with choppers and a ship to operate from to get us in and out of Romania without starting a war.

"So I need a Black Ops company, one like I use to command when I was serving in the army.

"As you know, I always want a superior force in numbers and weapons for any battle I'm going in. and with this type of operation I feel the same way.

"In the past I lost too many people in too many fights, where we were outnumbered and out gunned, I never intent to let it happen again."

"Tom, you know that type of company is hard to find available right now due to the wars we're fighting in Iraq and Afghanistan.

"You should be one of the first persons in the world to know how much there needed in the fights we're in."

"Don't you think I know it, but if we don't stop them, you may have more people killed in America then all of the wars for the past fifty years right in your own back yard and maybe you won't have a backyard anymore, because they may be targeting the CIA Headquarters?

"Besides if you get me the information on the site where our people are being held, maybe I can get them in and out in one night. Then all you will have to do is get the State Department to make peace with the Romania Government for our slight invasion of their country."

"All right Tom, I'll contact the pentagon and have them gather the intelligence using their spy satellites and make a few fly over's of the area with one of our spy planes, it shouldn't take more than a couple of days to gather the information for you."

"That's great Ron, but don't forget about my ship and my Black Ops Company!"

"Of course I won't forget about them. I'll call you when I have everything set-up for you."

"Thanks Ron."

Tom hung up his satellite phone and started thinking about his long lost love, after all these years he still couldn't get over losing her.

Tom tried never to talk about her or think about being tossed aside for someone else while he was fighting in Nam.

He loved his girl with all of his heart and no matter how hard he tried he still hadn't gotten over her. After her, he never even dated again.

He thought back to all of his friends who wanted to set him up with somebody, for God sake even his mother tried.

Tom wouldn't go out with any woman and thought he never would.

He took risk, so many risks as a soldier and a CIA Agent, the only thing he thought he didn't do was to take risk with other people's lives.

Tom had to get his mind back to the task at hand. He had a lot of people's lives at stake right here and right now.

He had to quit thinking about the past and begin planning how they would get their folks away from al-Qaeda without losing any of the hostages or the troops assigned to help him do this job.

Three days later Tom's satellite phone rang and Tom picked up the phone and said, "This is Tom Parker."

"Tom, this is Ron and you should have all of your pictures and information on the buildings where our people are being held in the morning, including the types of weapons al-Qaeda's men have."

"That's great Ron, how about my Black Ops and my ship."

"They're on their way to you and should be off the coast in two days, when they arrive in your area. I'll have them call you and you can make arrangements to be picked up and taken to the ship to do the planning for the assault of their camp."

"All right Ron, you did well!"

Two days later Tom received a call from Captain Jon Jones, Commander of the Aircraft Carrier America, advising Tom, they were about fifty miles off the coast almost directly east of his location.

Captain Jones wanted to know where they could pick him and his two agents up with one of their chopper's.

Tom advised him to give them about four hours to get to a beach north of Tulcea and when they arrived he would call him for a chopper to pick them up.

Captain Jones said, "I'll wait for your call and then we'll use your telephone signal to guide the chopper to pick you up."

"Thanks captain, I'm look forward to meeting you."

Tom rounded up Rick and Hank, who had been walking around the campgrounds where they had been staying for some time now.

Tom said, "Let's go, we need to be on the beach near Tulcea in about four hours from now, leave the camping gear here, we won't need it again or be coming back here."

Hank was thrilled about that, he'd had enough of camping and sleeping in the woods, he was a city boy through and through and wanted nothing ever again to have anything to do with camping or sleeping on a cot in the great outdoors.

Rick was happy to leave, even if it only meant he didn't have to pack up their gear again, he too, was used to sleeping in beds and never spent time roughing it in his entire life.

Tom didn't care one way or the other. He spent some many years in the army either training in the field or in combat in every kind of climate. He could survive wherever he was.

It didn't matter to him, not that he was against sleeping in a nice clean bed with a bathroom close by.

He could sleep almost anywhere if somebody wasn't shooting at him.

Some days, Tom wondered why he followed in his father's footsteps, his dad was a career military man who retired as a Major General, in the army and his dad's combat action in Korea won him the Medal of Honor, which insured Tom an appointment to West Point.

Tom graduated in the middle of his West Point Class and spent his life in the army, as either an intelligent officer or as a commander of a Special Forces Unit.

His work as an intelligent officer working with the CIA was the reason he was asked to join the company.

However, his service as a commander of a special force unit didn't hurt him either to become a CIA Agent.

He was a highly decorated combat commander with a couple of Distinguished Service Crosses; Distinguished Service Medal, two Purple Hearts, three Silver Stars and a Bronze Star and a ton of combat battle ribbons and a combat infantry badge.

The only major medal he didn't have was a Medal of Honor and he was glad he didn't have it, because other than his dad everyone he had ever know to receive it was killed in action wining it.

In addition to all his medals and ribbons he had many awards for shooting competitions held by the army. He was one of the top marksmen in the army and was an expert with every weapon he ever trained on.

Tom had been lucky in his career to have been appointed as a Lieutenant Colonel, by General Westmoreland when he was on his staff in Viet Nam to command a Special Forces Unit, even though he hadn't enough time in grade as a major for his promotion.

However, the general wanted a colonel to command this elite fighting force and the general got what he wanted.

When Tom finished his twenty years of service with the army and obtained his promotion to bird colonel, he took his retirement and joined the CIA the next day.

When Tom, Rick and Hank arrived on the coast, Tom called Captain Jones to tell him they were ready to be picked up.

The captain told him he had a chopper ready to pick them up and bring them to the carrier and it was on its way.

Tom, Rick and Hank waited on the beach where Tom had picked out a clear area for the chopper to land and a place out of sight of prying eyes.

They didn't have long to wait because after only about forty minutes Tom could hear the whirling blades of a helicopter coming in low over the ocean.

Tom said, "Rick, you and Hank better get your stuff ready to board the chopper because it's soon going to be her to pick us up and get us out of here."

Rick and Hank grabbed their gear out of the van; Tom had taken his out of the van when they arrived on the beach.

Sure enough within minutes the chopper's lights were lighting the beach like it was daylight and when the pilot saw Tom give him a thumbs up signal, he landed the chopper.

After the cloud of dust from the propellers cleared, Tom heard the pilot yell, "Get aboard so we can get out of here!"

Tom didn't need an engraved invitation; he jumped in the chopper as soon as a crew member opened the door with Rick close behind him.

It took Hank a bit to get up his nerve before he approached the open door of the chopper and climbed in after the crewman said, "Get your butt in here, we've got to get out of here!"

Hank kind of made a head first dive through the open doorway of the chopper and the moment he had his feet inside the door, the crewman closed the door and the pilot took off.

Hank was very nervous on the flight to the carrier, since he had never been in a chopper before and the sudden movements of the chopper from side to side had him going from one side of the ship to the other.

Thirty minutes past before the pilot had the chopper on the deck of the carrier and Tom thought Hank never was seated for the entire trip.

As soon as they landed on the carrier, they were taken to a meeting room where Captain Jon Jones and the commander of the Special Forces Unit, Colonel Ken Kincaid were waiting for them.

Tom introduced himself to them and proceeded to introduce Rick and Hank to the two men.

Colonel Kincaid said, "Colonel Parker, I served with you for a short time in the Gulf War and have to say I learned more about command than when I was at West Point from you.

"You were tough, but fair and you did everything possible to look after your people."

"That's very nice of you to say, but I'm sure you had a lot of good commander's while serving in the military."

"True, but none I learn so much from as I did from you."

"Ken, we've got a tough assignment right now to extract a bunch of folks from a mountain top, in a country that's probably not going to look kindly on us invading their country to save our seven people.

"So we better get started with our plans on how to get these people out of there as quickly and quietly as possible."

For the next two days, Tom and Ken went over the photo's learning everything about the location of the buildings, good landing spots for the troops and develop flight plans to get in and out of the area as quick and easy as possible.

Finally, they were ready with their plans to rescues' their scientists and they planned to do it tonight.

Ken met with his troops and detailed the plan to them and introduced CIA Agents, Tom Parker and Rick Byrd to the company and explained Tom Parker was in charge of this operation, so he gives you an order you follow it to the letter.

Ken also told his men Tom Parker is a highly decorated retired colonel that I learned more about combat then any officer I served with in the army.

That made the men, feel better about taking orders from a CIA Agent.

10

The next morning Chance came to after being hit on the head last night, his head hurt so bad, his arms were numb and he need to go to the bathroom.

He couldn't possibly get to his feet and he had PJ's dried blood all over his face. What did he do by trying to escape he got PJ killed.

Chance tried to holler for help, but realized he wasn't going to get any help from any of the guards and his friends would be shot if they tried to help. What could he do, just lay there in pain and hurt.

It seemed like hours and hours past after he woke up before anyone came downstairs to check on him, and when someone finally did, it was al-Sadr.

Al-Sadr unlocked his cell and came into the room and asked how he was feeling?

Very bad, Chance told him.

Al-Sadr asked, "Dr. Taylor are you ready to behave yourself and do the work I brought you here to do or do you plan to have me kill all of your friends.

"Next time, I promise you the next one of your friends killed will not have such an easy death as PJ had, and you my friend, will have a front row seat to their death.

"I asked you yesterday if you understood me, but apparently you didn't, you keep up your bad behavior and you will soon run out of friends.

"I'll ask you for the last time. Do you understand what I want and what I'm prepared to do, to get what I want?"

"I understand. No more problems with me."

"Good, I hope you mean it this time. I like your friends and they deserve better from you."

Al-Sadr called for some of the guards to come down and to help get Chance up and to take him upstairs to get him cleaned up.

After Chance had his head bandaged and a shower, clean clothes and a shave he came out to the dining room.

His friends all told him he had been stupid to try to escape and Curtis wouldn't even look at him. Chance didn't blame him.

He had been stupid all right, trying to escape to get help for his friends. He didn't know where he could have gone to get help, or who he could have trusted to help him?

Al-Sadr, took Chance and Charles to their new lab, and as al-Sadr had promised, everything they needed to assemble suitcase nuclear bombs were there.

Dr. Zortman was already at work when they arrived.

He was preparing timers to be used to set the bombs off and they were all to explode on the same date.

Zortman was an expert on all phases of nuclear bomb making, although maybe not quite as good as Chance and Charles in their narrow specialties, but he was good enough to know if they were doing their work right.

As they worked preparing ten bombs for al-Sadr to attack America, Chance faced a real dilemma. Should he cause the death of people he knew, his friends by failing to do the work on the bombs; or cause the death of thousands of people he didn't know?

He finally accepted the decision he made, to save the people he knew first and hoped he could find a way to save the ones he didn't know.

He talked to Charles to see what he thought about their dilemma. Charles told him we have to save our friends first.

It was surprising to Chance how quickly they managed to build ten suitcase bombs with the materials stolen from Russia.

Chance asked Zortman why he was involved with such a project just to hear what he would say, his answer was simple, five million dollars in gold bars.

In less than two weeks, the ten bombs were built and packed into a special shipping container and that night al-Sadr held a very special large party for all of the hostages.

One thing about al-Sadr, he didn't spare any expense on food for this party. The hostages had more than they could eat and drink.

Al-Sadr even had a glass of wine with them and was in high spirits telling them all how much he enjoyed having them as his guests.

Later that night al-Sadr and his men left with the container filled with ten suitcase nuclear bombs.

After the party was over and al-Sadr and his men left the Mountain Top Lodge the hostages went to bed fearing the worse.

Chance had been in bed about thirty minutes when his bedroom door opened quietly and someone came in the room.

Chance laid as quiet as he could when whoever had come in to his room came up right next to his bed.

Chance held his breath thinking the next thing he would hear was a gunshot or feel a knife cutting his throat, but instead of either of these things happening he heard, "Chance, are you awake?"

Chance sat straight up in bed, reached to turn on the light next to his bed, and when the light was turned on.

Chance saw Shannon standing next to the bed wearing her robe.

"God, Shannon you scared me. I thought they had come to my room to kill me since we finished making the bombs for al-Sadr."

"Chance, there something I've got to tell you before they kill us. I'm sure they plan to kill us since you've finished making the bombs for al-Sadr."

"What do you want to tell me?"

Shannon sat down on the side of Chance's bed and said, "Ever since I first saw you lying naked beside the stream. I've been thinking about you and wondering about how it would be making love with you."

"Is that what you came to say?"

"I guess it is, and the only reason I can say something like this now, is because I'm sure in the morning they're going to kill us.

"Otherwise, I would never have the nerve to say it to you. I don't want to die without knowing how it would be making love with you."

Chance reached for her, pulled her into his arms and kissed her and then said, "Shannon, I know this is crazy with everything that's happened to us since we met.

"I've been thinking about you and remembering sleeping in your tent with you lying next to me and wanting you so much it hurt."

"Chance, I don't want to die without making love with you."

Chance laid her down on the bed beside him and rolled over on top of her and begin kissing her and pulling the zipper down on her robe.

He was surprised when he found she had nothing on under her robe, his hands found her breasts and gently held them in his hands.

Then he rolled off of her and finished pulling the zipper down and helped her off with her robe. Well, she did have a little on under her robe, a pair of pink panties.

As she lay there on his bed looking at him with those big blue eyes, he realized how beautiful she was.

He began kissing her lips and slowly moved his kisses down her neck and continued down her body until he held those lovely breasts in his hands again.

He teased the nipple of each of her breasts with his tongue until she said, "Chance, I can't wait anymore. I need you in me, make love to me and do it now."

She reached down to take her panties off and Chance said, "Darling, let me help you."

He slowly pulled her panties down and as he was pulling them off he was studying every inch of her body, when her panties were down around her ankles.

He suddenly took his right hand and grabbed the crotch of her panties and jerked them completely off.

He moved slowly back up onto her body and kept telling her how much he wanted and needed her and she responded by spreading her legs apart, and pulled him closer to her until she felt him inside her.

They continued making love all through the night and by time daybreak came both of their bodies were completely satisfied and exhausted, and they were so much in love.

Chance said, "Shannon, this can't be the end for us, we've got to find a way out of here.

"I've got to find those bombs and disarm them. I don't want to be responsible for killing thousands of Americans. I've got to help find them!"

"Oh, Chance what can we do to get away from these people?"

"I don't know, but I'll think of something. I've got to!"

Shannon replied, "I know you can do it, you've got to!"

"Shannon, we need to get showered and get dressed for breakfast with our friends."

"I know we do, but I don't want to leave you for a moment, any moment could be our last one here on earth, they could kill us anytime."

"I know darling, but we still have to do what we can to stay alive and being present for breakfast is the first thing we have to do for the day."

They kissed each other hard and Shannon got out of bed found her pink panties and pulled them on and put on her robe.

Shannon kissed Chance one more time before she went out the door back to her room.

Forty-five minutes later they met in the hall at the same time Charles was coming out of his room. They exchanged greetings to each other like they just saw each other for the first time this morning.

Then they both said good morning to Charles.

Chance was certain they would all be killed as soon as al-Sadr left, but instead Charles and he were told to go back to the lab and keep building bombs until they ran out of material to build bombs with.

After al-Sadr left with the bombs, Chance had the opportunity to ask Zmitrovitch, why was he was helping al- Qaeda? These are the people who help fight against Russia in Afghanistan.

Like Zortman, he had a very simple answer, fifty million dollars in gold for me and my men, plus the opportunity to strike against America.

America may have won the cold war, but now is my chance to make them pay for all of my KGB comrades they killed and he could do it by using al-Qaeda and make himself rich at the same time.

Now, at least Chance understood why the Russians were helping terrorists, one of the oldest reasons in the world money, money, big money!

Chance still hadn't figured out how al-Qaeda knew to stop a ship on the high seas and take them captive, and why kill all of the crew members and sink the ship.

He also couldn't understand his friends, Charles and Anmend who seemed so willing to cooperate with al-Sadr.

Chance guessed Charles had to try to get home alive for his wife and girls, and Anmend was protecting his sister.

Al-Sadr and his men left Mountain Top Lodge under the care of Colonel Zmitrovitch and his men with orders after Drs. Taylor and Brown finished making as many bombs as they could, he was to kill all of the hostages.

Except the people whose name was on a list he gave to Zmitrovitch, these people he was to help leave with their things to go wherever they wanted to go.

He was to bury the last bombs they made in the location the two of them worked out a few weeks ago.

Last by not least, he was to burn the lodge to the ground and destroy the metal building and its contents.

Chance and Charles were beginning to run out of certain parts they needed to keep building bombs and were scrambling to find substitute parts to let them keep working on the project as long as possible.

Chance told Charles, we've got to keep working on these bombs, because I'm sure when we're out of material they're going to kill all of us.

Charles kept tell him, no I don't think al-Sadr would kill us, he told us if we helped him he would lets us all go.

Chance couldn't understand how Charles could be so naive or if he was just hopeful everything was going to turn out all right.

After dinner that evening all of the captives were sitting around the lodge's living room talking about their lives.

When Curtis told Chance he wanted him to know he forgave him about PJ's death. He understood Chance was only trying to get away to save them and it was al-Sadr who shot and killed PJ, not Chance.

This was the first time Curtis had spoken to him since PJ was killed.

Chance thanked him for what he said and he wanted Curtis to know how sorry he was that PJ was killed.

Around two o'clock in the morning, Chance heard gunfire and thought oh no, they're beginning to kill hostages.

He was worried about Shannon and thought he better try to get to her room.

However, Chance got down on the floor and then he could hear men shouting in English, and more, and louder gunfire.

Then the door to his room opened and Chance saw a soldier in full nighttime fighting gear, including night vision goggles, some type of weapon, and the most beautiful sight on earth, an American Flag on the shoulder of his uniform.

The soldier told him to stay on the floor, two more soldiers came into Chance's room and one of them asked, are you Dr. Chance Taylor?"

"Yes, I'm Chance Taylor."

The soldier took off his night vision goggles and said, "Dr. Taylor, I'm Tom Parker, with the CIA, and this is Rick Byrd, CIA.

"We're here with a Special Forces Unit to get you and your friends out of here."

They could hear more gunfire outside of the lodge, the gunfire continued for another twenty minutes, then it stopped.

Tom Parker suggested to Chance, he get dressed and he would check to see if the others were dressed and ready to go home.

By the time Chance was dressed and had gone into the living room. The rest of his friends were coming down the hallway into the living room.

When all of the hostages were assembled in the living room the Commander of the Special Forces Unit joined them, he took off his helmet and goggles and said, "Folks I'm Colonel Ken Kincaid, Commander of the Special Forces Unit and we are here to take you people home.

Which ones of you are Dr. Taylor and Dr. Brown?"

Chance replied, "Colonel Kincaid, I'm Chance Taylor."

Chance pointed at Charles and said, "This is Charles Brown."

Chance said "I'll introduce all of the others to you, "Anmend Soekarmo and his sister, Kerida Soekarmo; Annie Taylor; Curtis La Salle; and Shannon O'Hara.

"I'm sorry to say PJ Murphy, was shot and killed several weeks ago by the al-Qaeda leader, Dr. al-Sadr."

Tom Parker introduced himself to the group as well as Rick Byrd and explained even though they were dressed in military uniforms, they were CIA Agents assigned to find the nuclear scientists and their friends.

Kincaid said, "We need to start loading people in the helicopters to go back to our ship, that's waiting for us off of the coast."

Chance said, "Colonel, we need to get some nuclear weapons stored in the metal building behind the lodge and take them with us."

` "OK, can you show us where they are and help pack them so they can be transported?"

"Yes, Dr. Brown and I can, did you get all of the ex- KGB Agents who were guarding us?"

Tom said, "I thought you were being held by al-Qaeda?"

"We were, but they also had ex- KGB Agents helping them."

Kincaid asked Chance to lead them to the building with the bombs in it, so we can take them out of here.

Kincaid suggested to Dr. Brown, he could stay behind with the others, because there was no reason to take more people out in the woods while there was still a chance there might be some of the enemy left hiding.

Brown agreed to stay with the others.

Chance told Colonel Kincaid there is a lot of gold stolen from Kuwait stored in the basement of this building and we need to take it with us too.

Tom said, "This is getting more interesting all of the time."

Chance was leading Kincaid, Tom, Rick and several troopers from the Colonel's Special Forces Unit to the steel building, where he and Charles had been working.

He asked, "Did you kill Colonel Zmitrovitch and Dr. Zortman when you came in or do you know?"

Tom said, "Did you say, Colonel Zmitrovitch?"

"Yes."

"Are you sure it was him?"

"I only know what al-Sadr told us when he introduced him to us. He said he was Colonel Zmitrovitch, an ex- KGB operative."

Tom replied, "I haven't seen him in person, but I would know him from his picture, unless he has changed a lot since our last photo of him. He's a notorious KGB killer, like al-Sadr, is in al-Qaeda?

"Dr. Taylor, did you know al-Sadr is one of the most wanted terrorist in the world, there's a twenty-five million dollar reward out on him?"

"No, I had no idea."

"You're lucky he needed you, otherwise you would have been dead! He went to a lot of trouble to get you and Dr. Brown."

Kincaid said, "You better stay back doctor, until we secure this building."

Kincaid motioned for his troops to storm the building, but before they got any closer they came under fire from the building. Everyone hit the ground including Chance.

The fire fight continued for over an hour, than the firing halted.

Three of the Special Forces troopers were hit during the first burst of gunfire. They were quickly evacuated by medics back to the ship by helicopter.

At this moment it looked like a standoff. The people in the building were well fortified and the troopers had the building surrounded, so no one could get out.

Kincaid asked Chance if he thought if they hit the building with a rocket from one of their gunships if there was any chance one of the nuclear bombs might go off.

After thinking about how they had the bombs secured he didn't think there was any chance of that happening.

The Colonel asked him if he was 100% sure.

He was!

Kincaid called out to the men inside the building and told them they had five minutes to surrender or he was calling in rockets to take out the building.

A few minutes past when Kincaid yelled out, you've got one minute.

From inside the building they heard, OK we're coming out. Bright lights were turned onto the building by Kincaid's troops as the people inside came filling out.

The first person out of the building was Colonel Zmitrovitch, followed by Dr. Zortman and six other men.

The Special Forces troopers immediately had all of the men laying face down on the ground and placed plastic straps on their wrists, with their hands behind their back.

Chance knew all about having his hands strapped behind his back like that, he knew it hurt like hell.

The troopers helped the men up from the ground, searched them for hidden weapons and begin moving the prisoners back toward the lodge.

Two troopers carefully checked the building to be certain none of the enemy was still hiding in the building. Before allowing Chance and the others in, now they indicted the building was clear.

Chance showed Kincaid where the nuclear bombs were.

Kincaid, gave orders to his men to move the bombs to the lodge to be ready to load them in their helicopters Arriving at the lodge Zmitrovitch and Zortman were separated from the others.

They would be taken to Istanbul by the CIA for questioning.

The other men would be questioned by the military on their ship waiting in the Black Sea for the troopers to return from their mission.

Tom introduced himself and Rick to Colonel Zmitrovitch and told him. "I've heard so much about you. I look forward to talking with you at length."

Zmitrovitch responded, "I'm sorry, I've never heard of you or Rick. I would shake hands with you, but they're a little tied up at the moment."

Tom thought the colonel was as cool of a customer as he had ever seen in his life.

Helicopters begin landing in front of the lodge, the troopers loaded their prisoners in one of them and secured them with cables attached to their plastic straps and the cables attached to the floor of the helicopter.

Next, the nuclear bombs were loaded in one of the helicopters and the gold in three others.

Finally, they started loading the freed hostages into helicopters, along with the troopers.

The last helicopter loaded contained the two special prisoners, Zmitrovitch and Zortman, in addition to Chance, Tom, Rick, and Kincaid and four of his troopers.

Arriving on the aircraft carrier the hostages were greeted as hero's by the crew of the carrier.

The three wounded troopers had been taken to sick bay, before the last of the helicopters arrived on the deck of the carrier.

As soon as the helicopter with Chance landed, he was introduced to Hank Sollenberger.

Tom told Chance without Hank you folks would have never been found.

Tom said, "Hank is a CIA theorist and analysis, who came up with the idea of a terrorist plot after reading about a reported break-in at a Russian Nuclear Lab and later about the Panama Star sinking with two American Nuclear Scientists on-board.

"He reasoned there must be a connection.

"So, without CIA approval, he hired a salvage company to find the wreckage of the Panama Star and they located eleven crew members, who had been executed by being shot in the head.

"Finding those men set off a search to find you and your friends. Then Hank found a Gypsy Fortune Teller, who knew your name and her brother knew where you went, that information allowed us to find you and come and get you and your friends."

Chance, thanked Hank for saving his life and saving the lives of his friends and he guessed.

He should give Juanita and Michael a lot of thanks for their helping in saving him and his friends.

Chance said, "We have another major problem, al-Sadr left with ten suitcase nuclear bombs several days ago with plans to set them off in America."

Hank said, "You mean he has ten suitcase nuclear bombs enroute to America?"

"Yes, and we got to stop him before it's too late."

11

Al-Sadr and his men traveled to Varna, Bulgaria by truck, along with a small container of ten suitcase nuclear bombs neatly packed inside it. From Varna they traveled on a ferry boat to Istanbul, Turkey.

Arriving in Istanbul al-Sadr left his men and his container to fly ahead to get things ready for the arrival of his container.

His men would repack the small container into a larger container filled with Turkish Rugs, than they would travel on a freighter with the container to Amsterdam.

There the men would stay in Europe and the container would be shipped on to Montreal, Canada to Dr. J. Robert Oppenheimer, an aliases being used by al-Sadr.

Al-Sadr flew from Istanbul to London, where he stayed for a few days holding meetings with the London al-Qaeda cell leader.

From London he took a flight directly to Montreal. After arriving in Montreal he began contacting al-Qaeda members in the United States and Canada and told them a code phrase to authenticate it was actually al-Sadr contacting them, the phrase was "it's time to see the doctor" then he gave them an address in Montreal and a time of their appointment.

He made ten calls and either told the person who answered the phone the message or asked it be given to his agent, or he left the message on a telephone recorder.

Next, he sit out to purchase a group of used vehicles of various types, ages and makes, he purchased a Chevrolet Tahoe, a thirty-five foot motor home, a Ford super cab pickup, Dodge pickup with a fifth wheel trailer, Chrysler Minivan, Lincoln Stretch Limo, Toyota Land Cruiser, Nissan SUV, Fifteen Passenger School Bus and an old pick-up with a slide in camper.

Then he had two Montreal al-Qaeda members build ten false fuel tanks to hold the suitcase nuclear bombs in that could be fitted onto each of the vehicles.

He then purchased an additional fuel tank for each vehicle that they could actually put fuel in.

In mid August his agents begin arriving in Montreal, he had each agent staying in a different hotel or motel in the Montreal area.

He never let any of them meet. He individually gave each of them training on their assignment and had them pick up the vehicle they had been assigned in a different place in the City.

The agents were from ten different cities in either America or Canada, so there was no chance they knew one another and he made sure they never met.

This way if one of his men were caught by the Americans, they could never give any information about any of the other terrorists to them.

Al-Sadr had all of the vehicles registered by the driver assigned to the vehicle in Quebec and had each of them purchase their own insurance for their vehicles.

Next, he gave each of the drivers their assignments:

Each driver was given his assignment, along with giving them a target and a location to cross the border and the vehicle assigned to their target:

The old pick-up with slide-in camper in Boston's the John F. Kennedy Federal Building and they were to cross the border at Quebec City, Quebec.

Chevrolet Tahoe, the New York Stock Exchange and their border crossing was at Montreal.

Fifteen Passenger School Bus target was the White House, border crossing at Landsdown, Ontario.

Chrysler Minivan, Independence Hall, border crossing at, Niagara Falls, Ontario.

Toyota Land Cruiser the Sears Tower crossing the board at Windsor, Ontario.

Dodge pickup with fifth wheel trailer the target, New Orleans' French Quarter, border crossing at Sault Ste. Marie, Ontario.

Ford Super Cab, the target was DFW Airport Terminal Two East, border crossing at Thunder Bay, Ontario.

Thirty-five foot motor home the target was Caesar's Palace, border crossing at Coutts, Alberta.

Nissan SUV target was the Golden Gate Bridge, border crossing at Kingsgate, British Columbia.

Lincoln Stretch Limo target was the Los Angeles City Hall, border crossing at White Rock, British Columbia.

Al-Sadr expected a success ratio for exploding the nuclear bombs of say, 40% after all he couldn't expect all ten of the bombs to make it through to their targets.

However, four nuclear bombs exploding on the same day in America would be a real victory for al-Qaeda, it would be enough.

All of his agents now had their assignments and were waiting only for his shipment to arrive.

The ship was due to dock in Montreal on August 25th, the port officials told Dr. Oppenheimer, it would take two to three days for his container to clear customs, but he should have his container no later than August 30th.

Al-Sadr contacted a custom clearance agent and gave him copies of his shipping documents for his Turkish Rugs, purchased on his recent trip to Istanbul.

Dr. Oppenheimer said his wife was very anxious to get her new rugs for a party she was having in early September.

The custom agent said he knew all about problems with wives expecting something for a special occasion and assured him he would give his shipment priority service.

August 25th, al-Sadr telephoned the office of the shipping company to see if the freighter arrived this morning from Amsterdam and wanted to know if they could check to see if the container he was expecting arrived on their ship.

He was told the ship had docked a few minutes ago, but they had not received the shipping papers for all of the freight that's in the process of being unloaded. Perhaps if he called back later today, they could tell him about his container.

Al-Sadr thanked them for their help and said he would call back later in the day.

He called the shipping company back late in the afternoon and was told they now had all of the shipping documents for the freight unloaded from the ship.

The shipping company clerk asked who the container was shipped to and al-Sadr said, "Dr. J. Robert Oppenheimer."

The clerk told him to please hold on and he would check, yes, the container had arrived and his custom agent had already picked up the papers and was working to get the shipment cleared by Canadian Customs.

The next day al-Sadr called the custom agent to see how long it would be before his shipment would be cleared?

The agent said, "I've just returned from clearing your container and you can pick it up anytime from dock 34. You will need to stop by my office and get your papers before going to pick up the container."

Al-Sadr told the agent he would be there as soon as he could get a truck and some men to help him.

One hour later, al-Sadr picked up his custom documents, paid the customs agent fee and the import duties on the Turkish Rugs and drove a truck with three men to dock 34.

A few minutes later the container was loaded onto the truck and driven to a storage building, the men unloaded the container into the storage building, al-Sadr paid the men in cash for their time and for using their truck.

Then he begin calling his al-Qaeda agents to set-up appointments for them to come and pick up their packages, one at a time, he had his helpers who made the false fuel tanks standing by to load the suitcases into the fuel tanks of the vehicles.

Al-Sadr, first started with the agents assigned to the targets in the Western United States to pick up their cases, the ones which had the farthest to travel.

The LA agent was first, followed by San Francisco, one city after another until five days later all ten of the agents and their vehicles were enroute to their targets in America.

After the last of the vehicles left Montreal enroute to their destinations, al-Sadr shot and killed the two men who built the false gas tanks and who installed them onto the vehicles to be sure they could not give any information about the vehicles to anyone.

He placed their bodies inside the empty container. Then he went to Dorval, Montreal's International Airport and boarded a plane to Mexico City via Dallas.

After arriving in Mexico City he stayed for three days and then purchased a ticket to Buenos Aires, Argentina.

Al-Sadr already began formulating plans for how he could strike America as he traveled to Buenos Aires. He needed to come up with something, something that would shake Americans so bad. They would even lose confidents in their government and maybe something that might effective their daily life.

Americans loved eating, maybe he could find something which would affect their food supply, yeah, and he loved it! Now all he had to do was figure out what?

12

Arriving in Istanbul the CIA spend hours and hours, grilling not only Colonel Zmitrovitch and Dr. Zortman, but all of the people who had been hostages.

Hank Sollenberger sit in on a lot of the interrogations of the prisoners and their captives.

The same questions kept coming to his mind how did, al-Qaeda know about the ship the scientists were traveling on, and how did they know where the ship was for them to take the scientists off of the ship in the middle of an ocean.

Hank surmised one of the hostages had to be involved in the plot and had provided information to al-Qaeda about the ship, but how?

Hank talked to Tom Parker and asked him if he thought it was possible for one of the hostages to have been involved in the plot, maybe, was Tom's answer.

So far the only things they knew for sure, was the operation was under the control of al-Sadr and that Chance and Charles,

built eighteen nuclear bombs and ten of them left with al-Sadr for targets in America.

Tom was sure Zmitrovitch and Zortman didn't know any more about al-Sadr's targets in America then they did.

Their big concern was staying prisoners of the United States and not being sent to Russia for the crime of stealing nuclear materials, among many others charges they faced if they returned to Russia, each of the charges in Russia would mean execution for them.

Hank continued to think about what would be common to all of the hostages and what would be with all of them on the trip, because the only hostage who wasn't on the Panama Star was Shannon O'Hara.

Hank concluded only one thing was common to all of them, Chance's car, they would always be with the car, maybe something had been attached to the car to let al-Qaeda, know where the car was and then they would know where the scientists were.

Hank, found Luke Turner was still working off of the Greek Island of Samothraki, he got Luke on the radio and asked him if he and his crew could go back to the Panama Star and see if they could recover the Chevrolet Corvette or as much of it as possible to see if there was some type of tracking device on it.

He could and he would, Luke told Hank he would pick him up in Istanbul, in the morning and they would go back to the sunken ship and see what they could do to find the Corvette.

It didn't take them long to find the Corvette, it was still in its crate, somehow when the second explosion ripped the ship apart, the crate slipped out of the sinking ship and settled on the bottom of the ocean floor all by its self.

The divers soon had cables on the crate and the recovery ship's winch pulled the crate up and swung the car onto the deck of the ship.

Hank thought Chance, was never going to believe it, the car still had the plastic wrap covering it and after the crew, used water hoses to spray off the mud and gunk from the ocean, the car looked to be in pretty good condition.

At that point Hank, asked Luke to take him and the car back to Istanbul so the CIA folks could go over the car.

Arriving back in Istanbul the CIA took possession of the Corvette and had it moved to a warehouse, where they had a team of investigators remove the plastic material from the car and put the car up on a lift, so they could look under it and after several hours they found a black box which appeared not to be part of the car.

They carefully opened the box and found it contained a tracking device that used the GPS satellite system, for someone to be able to find the car's location, something like the ones used by companies in America to find stolen cars, only slightly more complex.

When the black box was given to Tom, he and Rick started questioning, Annie Taylor, with Hank observing, they asked her if she went completely over the Corvette in Albuquerque, she told them she went over every piece of the car.

Tom took the black box out of a paper carton and threw it on the table in front of her and asked, what's this thing we found on the Corvette?

Annie looked at the box and replied, "I don't know, but it doesn't have anything to do with the Corvette. What are you people trying to pull you bring out some kind of a black box and ask me what it is.

"If it was on the Corvette you people must have put it there, it sure wasn't there when I checked over the car. So what is it?"

Tom continued, "Annie, are you tell me you checked over the car and you never saw this box?"

"I've never seen this box in my life."

"You must not have looked over the car very well, since our people found this box attached under the car."

"I don't believe it!"

"You better believe it, how long have you be involved with al-Qaeda and why would you help them?"

"Are you out of your mind? I not involved with al-Qaeda or anybody else except General Motors."

"Annie, are you trying to say General Motors is involved with al-Qaeda?"

"You people are nuts! General Motors and I are not involved with al-Qaeda, you guys are crazy and another thing, when are you going to let me talk to my parents to let them know I'm alive?"

"OK, let's stop for a minute, if you didn't have anything to do with putting the black box on the car, who else had access to the car when you're getting it ready to ship?"

"I don't know it wasn't being guarded when it was in Albuquerque, Chance came over when I was working on the car, Charles, Kerida and

Anmend were all there at sometime during the time I was working on the car.

I even had some local Chevy mechanics helping me work and check the car over."

"OK, Annie you can go back to your room, but don't talk to anyone about our conversation."

"Who am I going to talk to you've had us locked up by ourselves like we're prisoners every since we arrived in Istanbul. We're being treated worse by you guys, then when we were being held by al-Qaeda."

Tom didn't give her an answer and another CIA agent took her back to her room.

After she left the room, Tom said, "I don't think she has anything to do with it."

Rick and Hank agreed.

They questioned Chance next, he asked when they showed him the black box, what is it?

They questioned all of the hostages who had been rescued and generally got the same reaction.

After they had talked to each of them, Tom asked Hank, "What he thought and did he think one of them was lying?"

Hank told Tom and Rick, "Yes I do, but the problem I have is. I don't know which one."

They continue to question the hostages and the prisoners for several more days and were getting nowhere.

The CIA kept the story of the hostages rescue out of the media and hadn't allowed any of them to contact their families or anyone else.

They didn't want to tip off al-Sadr they were on his trail.

Hank reasoned al-Sadr must have transported the nuclear bombs to Istanbul in order to send the bombs by ship to America, the CIA requested help from the Turkish Police to obtain copies of all shipping documents for every shipment leaving Istanbul for the past four weeks.

When Hank was not listening to the questioning of the hostages or the prisoners, he was going through shipping documents.

After going through hundreds of documents, he found the one shipment he felt was the one he was looking for.

He grabbed the document and ran to find Tom and Rick.

Hank said, "I found it. I know I have. I found the bombs."

Tom asked, "What makes you think so?"

"Look who this shipment of Turkish Rugs are shipped to."

Tom and Rick looked at the document Hank was shoving in their face, the document read, one container, contents: Turkish Rugs, shipped to Dr. J. Robert Oppenheimer; Montreal, Canada and marked "Hold for Dr. Oppenheimer's Arrival."

Tom said, "What makes, you think this is our bombs?"

"Don't you know or remember who Dr. J. Robert Oppenheimer was?

"He was the father of the Atom Bomb."

"By God, you're right!"

Tom called in his boss, Chief Richard Queen and told him what Hank had discovered.

Chief Queen immediately sent a Flash Message to CIA Headquarter in Langley to alert them and to have agents check on the shipment of Turkish Rugs shipped to Dr. J. Robert Oppenheimer in Montreal.

Tom said, "We need to get to Montreal as soon as we can and take Drs. Taylor and Brown with us to be able to disarm the bombs if we can find them."

Two hours later Hank, Chance, Charles, Tom and Rick were on an Air Force Jet winging their way to Montreal to meet the CIA agents who were dispatched from Washington DC to see what they can find out about the shipment of Turkish Rugs.

They're only hope was they could intercept the shipment before Dr. al-Sadr could claim it.

13

Arriving in Montreal, the group from Istanbul met with the group from Washington and Hank was surprised to find Beverly Jenkins and Ron Parsons heading up the investigation.

By the time Hank and his group arrived in Montreal, Ron Parsons and the Washington agents had found the shipment of Turkish Rugs cleared customs six days ago and despite help from the Royal Canadian Mounted Police, no sign or even a clue of Dr. J. Robert Oppenheimer could be found.

The custom agent who cleared the container for him said he had never met him before and he paid his fee and the custom duties on the rugs in cash.

The one thing they know for sure was al-Sadr had control of the nuclear bombs on the North America Continent, the question was, where were al-Sadr and the bombs?

Ron Parsons turned to Hank and said, "OK Hank, you've been right about this plot from the beginning, so where is al- Sadr, and what has he done with the bombs?"

"If I was him I would have planned my targets long before ever getting the bombs and would have known how I would deliver them to my targets.

"Then I would go to South America and not be anywhere near them."

"Assuming you're right, what would his targets be and how would he deliver the bombs to the sites?"

"I would pick high profile targets, targets the world would recognize. So they knew al-Qaeda was still in the game and was a major player, they need to keep getting money and recruits and that's how they can do it."

Ron said, "Name ten?"

"The White House, the New York Stock Exchange, targets like that."

"So how would you get ten bombs to those kinds of targets from Montreal?"

"Ron, you have to remember these bombs aren't very big, they're in suitcases.

"Drs. Taylor and Brown have told us the size of them and everything about them since they assembled them."

"You still haven't told me how you would get ten bombs through customs between Canada and the United States."

"First, I would never plan that all ten bombs would make it to their targets.

"I'd guess Dr. al-Sadr figured less than half would get to their targets. If I was planning this operations. I would conceal them somehow in vehicles to cross over the border and I would have the vehicles crossing at ten different border locations into the United States."

"All right Hank, if you were concealing the bombs in vehicles how would you go about it?"

"I would probably make some kind of false floor, maybe a compartment under the trunk of the vehicle."

"What kind of vehicle should we be looking for?"

"Different makes and types, but all large vehicles."

"Can't you make it easier for us by having all of these vehicles a like?"

"No, that's part of the beauty of my plan.

"I'm going to have all different types of vehicles and send them to different border crossings and to targets all across America, so you can't concentrate your efforts to protect the targets."

"All right Hank, what can we do to find what kinds of vehicles we are looking for?"

"Ask the Royal Canadian Mounted Police to pull up records for all vehicles purchased and registered over the last four weeks in Montreal, then narrow the search to large vehicles and hope we can figure out which vehicles al-Sadr is using for the operation."

Beverly said, "Ron, I think we better do what Hank suggest. He's been right about all of this so far."

Ron contacted the RCMP Commander of Montreal and requested his help in obtaining the information on all vehicles purchased and licensed in Montreal over the past four weeks.

Then he asked him if he could have the computer sort out only the large vehicles purchased during the time frame, vehicles at least the size of pickup truck.

The commander told him he would have his computer whizzes get started on it right away.

Two hours past and the RCMP commander called back and said he had a print-out for him on all vehicles purchased and licensed in Montreal over the past four weeks along with a sort of all vehicles pickup size or larger.

The information was enroute to their office as they were speaking.

Ron thanked him and said, "We may need a lot more of your help very soon to try to locate some of these vehicles."

The commander said, "I understand, just let me know what we can do."

Then they got two breaks to come their way, the first one was Richard Queen, CIA Chief of Istanbul send a Flash Message to Langley to say they got some information from Dr. Zortman for a deal if they didn't send him back to Russia.

Dr. Zortman told him the bombs were all programmed to explode on 9-11.

Hank said, "That figures, al-Qaeda wants to celebrate their destruction of the twin towers and the damage to the Pentagon."

The next break they got was information taking from a computer disk from an al-Qaeda computer expert arrested in London by MI-5.

On his disk were the ten targets in America approved by bin Laden for al-Sadr terrorist operation.

Ron asked to have the list of targets sent to him in Montreal. When the list of targets arrived the people seated around a large conference table became very sober when Ron read the list:

The White House: Independence Hall: John F. Kennedy Federal Building in Boston: New York Stock Exchange: Sears Tower, Chicago:

LA City Hall: Golden Gate Bridge: DFW Airport: The French Quarter, New Orleans and Caesar's Palace, Las Vegas.

Ron said, "People we now know the targets and the date of the attack, we've got to find and defuse these bombs before they can be detonated. Let's get to work."

Hank said, "Ron, one thing we could do is to stop all vehicles on the list by sending the vehicle's licenses numbers, make and model of the vehicles on the print-out of large vehicles and stop any of them from trying to cross the border into the USA."

"Great idea, I'll call the commander of the RCMP and have him meet with me and ask him to give the order to not allow any of the vehicles on this list to cross the border and to hold the vehicle and occupants of the vehicle until we clear them."

Thirty minutes past before the print-out of all vehicles on the list were sent to every border crossing between Canada and The United States and with orders to hold the vehicles and their occupants.

Ron asked, "What is today date?"

Beverly replied, "September 9th."

"That means we got two days to find all ten of these vehicles, we need to get the same list of vehicle information to every state in the US to get the police and highway patrol looking for these vehicles."

Beverly said, "OK, Ron I'm on it."

Beverly took a copy of the list and left the conference room to send out an all points bulletin to all law enforcement agencies in the United States.

Ron told Drs. Taylor and Brown, they had better get some rest because it didn't look like they would be getting much rest over the next two days if we have any luck finding the bombs.

Before they left the conference room the RCMP commander called to say they had one of the vehicles on the list at Landsdown, Ontario.

Ron gave instructions to Tom and Rick to go with the RCMP commander in his helicopter and take Drs. Taylor and Brown with them to defuse the bomb if they found one in the vehicle.

An hour and an half later, the helicopter landed at the border crossing, just Southwest of Landsdown, they could see agents searching a fifteen passenger bus.

The driver of the bus was handcuffed and sitting on the floor of the border station, everything from the interior of the bus had already been removed including the seats and they found nothing.

The agents on-site told them they had a wrecker coming to take the vehicle to the nearest station with a lift large enough to hold the bus, so they could get underneath it.

The wrecker arrived, the bus was attached to it and all of the agents loaded into cars, including Tom's crew, they followed the wrecker pulling the bus with RCMP vehicles leading the way.

Once inside the garage they put the bus up on a lift rack and begin examining the undercarriage of the bus, it took only a few minutes for the agents to locate a new looking fuel tank, it took only a few minutes more for them to remove the tank as fuel poured out of the tank onto the floor.

The decision was made to cut open the seams of the fuel tank, but first they drained all of the fuel out of the tank and filled it with water, they were surprised it took such a small amount of water to fill the tank.

When they cut the seams with a torch and removed the top of the tank. They found why a fuel tank that size required such a small amount of water to fill it, the tank had two compartments, one for the fuel and one for a suitcase.

Chance said, "You found one of the bombs."

Tom quickly called Ron Parsons to tell him they found one of the bombs and how the bomb was concealed in an auxiliary fuel tank.

Chance and Charles set about deactivating the bomb. When they had finished deactivating the bomb Chance remarked, one down nine to go.

The RCMP had a HazMat vehicle standing by to take the nuclear bomb to a safe storage location, the Canadian and US Governments would have to fight over who controlled the nuclear bomb at a later date.

Chance told Tom he should have Ron Parsons contact Sandia and get some additional nuclear scientists put on alert to help disarm the bombs.

Chance could draw them a diagram showing them the quickest and easiest way to deactivate the bomb so they wouldn't have to spend time deciding how to do it.

Tom thought it was a good idea and called Ron Parsons back and told him of Chance's suggestion.

Ron thought it was an excellent idea and in addition to the scientists at Sandia he would contact and have on alert, nuclear scientists from Oak Ridge and White Sands to be ready to help disarm the bombs using Chance's diagram.

Chance quickly sketched out a diagram of the steps required to deactivate the bombs and gave it to Tom.

Tom had it faxed to Ron from the truck repair garage, where they had opened the fuel tank and found the bomb.

Back on the helicopter enroute back to Montreal, they received a radio message a Toyota Land Cruiser had been stopped trying to cross the border at Windsor and it was equipped with a new looking auxiliary fuel tank.

The RCMP commander instructed the vehicle to be taken to a repair garage, where the fuel tank could be removed and cut the tank open and he would arrive with the team to deactivate the bomb as soon as they could get there.

Enroute to Windsor the commander received another radio message that Sault Ste. Marie was holding a Dodge pickup with a fifth wheel trailer.

Again, he gave the officials at the border crossing the same instructions on what to do with the vehicle.

Ron Parsons called the commander and told him he was having an Air Force jet enroute to Windsor to pick up his team to get them to Sault Ste. Marie as soon as they had finished in Windsor.

The commander suggested to Ron he should have a jet pick up the bomb disposal team at Toronto, because it was going to take them too long to fly to Windsor in the helicopter.

The commander said "He would have another helicopter standing by to take them directly to the garage on their arrival in Windsor."

Ron told the commander, he would have an Air Force Jet standing by in Toronto for their arrival.

The bomb disposal team arrived in Toronto and boarded the Air Force jet for Windsor.

A second helicopter was waiting for them on their arrival in Windsor and ferried them quickly to the garage, where the bomb had already been removed from the fuel tank.

Chance and Charles quickly disarmed the second bomb and were back on the helicopter enroute to their Air Force jet.

The Air Force jet got top priority for takeoff and the team was enroute to Sault Ste. Marie.

On arrival in Sault Ste. Marie the same scenario took place; a helicopter was waiting to take them to another garage where the bomb had already been removed from the fuel tank and they disarmed it and then they were on their way back to the Air Force jet.

Chance and Charles got quicker at disarming the bombs with each one they did.

The next vehicle was a Ford Super Cab at Thunder Bay; their Air Force jet flew them directly across Lake Superior from Sault Ste. Marie to Thunder Bay.

Again, everything was ready for them on their arrival, bomb four disarmed.

Arriving back at the plane Chance wondered which port of entry would be next on their list.

He didn't have long to wait, they received a message from Ron Procter, they had a thirty-five foot motor home at Coutts, Alberta with a new auxiliary fuel tank, the vehicle was already enroute to a garage in Lethbridge and so were they.

Hank told Ron Parsons, I would send a nuclear scientists team from White Sands to Vancouver to be ready to disarm a couple of bombs at one or two of the border crossings in British Columbia.

Ron agreed and dispatched a team from White Sands to be standing by in Vancouver, when and if the RCMP border patrol found another of their vehicles.

Before the scientists arrived in Vancouver they got word the Kingsgate, British Columbia border patrol had a Nissan SUV with a new auxiliary fuel tank.

Ron told Hank, "You've been right at every turn on this operation, right now we've got six of the ten vehicles and their bombs.

So Hank, where do you think the other vehicles are at?"

"I think the pattern I see is, we've got one more vehicle that's going to try to cross the border somewhere in Western Canada and three vehicles that have already crossed the border and are somewhere in the Eastern part of America.

"We need to get a lot of eyes on the highways and streets in New York State and New England and we need to notify all of the police departments of the vehicles, we've caught so they take them off of the wanted list we sent out earlier."

Ron told Beverly to have a new list prepared eliminating the vehicles we've got and send the revised list to all law enforcement authorities in New York State and New England.

In addition, Ron contacted Oak Ridge and requested a team of nuclear scientists to go to New York City, to be in position to disarm bombs that might be found in the Northeastern section of the USA.

A team had been standing by in case they were needed and were soon airborne to New York City.

The Maine State Police found an old pick up with a slide-in camper parked alongside the road, just outside Kennebunkport on Interstate 95.

The driver was changing a flat tire. The vehicle license plate was on the list of vehicles wanted.

The driver put up no resistance and the vehicle was moved to a repair garage in Portland.

The scientists who had been enroute to New York City were now rerouted to Portland.

After Chance and Charles disarmed the bomb in Coutts, they were on their way to New York City.

While their plane was over North Dakota, they got word the New York State Police had stopped a Chevy Tahoe on Interstate 87 near Kingston, New York and found one of the new auxiliary fuel tanks.

The vehicle was impounded there and the driver was now in custody. Time was beginning to be a factor. It was now September 10th around ten-thirty PM, Eastern Daily Time.

The team in Maine would have to take care of the bomb in New York, because they were too far away from Kingston to get there in time.

Ron asked Hank, "We've got eight of the ten vehicles, so where are the other two?"

"I've been studying the locations of where each of the vehicles tried or crossed the border and I think I know the target for each one of those vehicles.

"By comparing my analysis to the information of the targets taken from the computer disc MI-5 found in London. I believe the two targets left are Independence Hall in Philly and Los Angeles City Hall.

We've got to double our efforts around those building right now!"

Ron called FBI Headquarters and requested they move at once to assist local police departments in Philadelphia and Los Angeles to cover the area around Independence Hall and the LA City Hall.

He told them he wanted them covered like they were under a blanket.

After Ron was off of the phone.

Hank told him he was going to look through the list of the other vehicles not on the large vehicles list to see if any of the vehicles on the complete list might fit the al-Qaeda purpose for delivering the bombs.

Hank suggested they should see if they could get a list of all vehicles that crossed the border at Niagara Falls; Grand Forks; Osoyoos; and White Rock, with Quebec license plates in the last two to three days.

If they could get those license plate numbers then they could compare them with the recent purchased vehicles and that should give them a clue of the other two vehicles they were looking for.

Hank begin studying the long list of recently licensed vehicles in Montreal to see if any of them stuck out as possible vehicles they should be looking for.

It was now almost four o'clock in the morning on September Eleventh, 9-11 a very bad date for America.

After spending two hours studying the list of vehicles, Hank received the list of vehicles with Quebec license plates crossing the border at the four crossing he asked for.

He found one of the license plates number in his list of vehicles crossed the border at Niagara Falls, a Chrysler Minivan.

Hank screamed at Ron to get an all points look out for the Chrysler Minivan in New York and Pennsylvania.

Ron had already routed the Air Force jet carrying Chance and Charles to Philadelphia with a helicopter standing by to whisk them to anyplace the bomb could be found.

Chance and Charles arrived in Philly and were sitting in the helicopter waiting for any word on the vehicle carrying the bomb destined for Independence Hall.

The problem they had was no one knew what time the bombs were set to go off, Dr. Zortman was still negotiating with the CIA for a better deal and although he gave them the date. He set the bombs to go off he hadn't given them the time.

14

hance knew only one thing whether the bombs got to their target or not, they would do unbelievable damaged to America. If they couldn't get the last two bombs disarmed.

They had to find these bombs.

State and local Police in New York and Pennsylvania were continually broadcasting to the public and to their patrol unit's information on the Silver Chrysler Minivan with Quebec License Plates.

As Chance and Charles sit waiting for any information on the minivan. Charles was visible upset, he told Chance they got to find those last two bombs, do you realize how much damage they could do and how many people could be killed and wounded?

Chance tried to comfort him, as tears began rolling down Charles cheeks, but Chance's comforting was not easing Charles emotional state.

Charles said through his tears, "What if the bomb sent to Chicago had gone off and my girls would have anywhere near Sears Tower, they would have been killed."

"Charlie, we stopped that bomb, your girls are save."

"Yeah my girls are save, but how about other people's little girls in Philadelphia if we can't find that bomb?"

Chance was getting ready to answer, when the pilot of the helicopter got a radio message that the minivan had been found, it had been involved in a terrible accident on Interstate I-476 South of Allentown.

The van was on fire and lying on its side after been hit by a semi truck, the driver of the van was dead. Fire trucks were on the scene and had the fire under control.

Traffic was stopped in both directions with debris covering all four lanes of the Interstate Highway.

Chance told Tom you need to contact the police and have them get a welder to the scene of the accident right now to cut into the fuel tank, so we can get to the bomb to disarm it.

We don't have time to have the van moved to a garage, since it's already September 11th and we don't know what time the bombs were set to go off.

By the time they arrived on the scene, a welder was standing by waiting for instructions on what he was supposed to do.

Chance ran out of the helicopter as soon as it touched down and showed the welder where he needed the auxiliary fuel tank cut opened.

The tank had received some damage from the wreck and the fire had it distorted; twisted and a mess.

The welder asked Chance if he thought it was save to begin cutting the metal with the torch or if the fuel tank might still have fuel in it.

Chance saw a rupture in the nozzle leading into the tank and burn marks all around it.

The decision was made the tank probably didn't have any fuel left in it. The welder begin cutting and it was a slow go, since he had to cut a lot more metal away before they could get access to the bomb and when they did the suitcase exterior had been burned and the lead lining of the case had fused into the bomb.

Chance now had to make a decision whether to risk torching the lead to get to the trigger and the timing device or hope there was so much damaged the bomb couldn't go off.

Chance called out for Charles, who was still having real emotional problems. Tom ran back to the helicopter and took Charles by the arm and pulled him out of the helicopter and literally dragged him to the crash site.

Chance said, "Charles quick what do you think, do we risk melting away the lead from the bomb, so we can disarm it or hope it can't go off with the lead in the firing mechanism and the timing device."

Charles heisted answering Chance's question.

"Come on Charles think, what should we do?"

Finally Charles replied, "Chance you can't take the chance the bomb won't go off, you got to get the lead away from the bomb."

Chance said, "I agree, Mr. Welder you've got to get the lead melted away from the bomb."

"Are you sure that's not going to set the bomb off?"

"Trust me it's not going to fire the bomb."

Carefully the welder began melting away the lead where Chance was pointing.

The bomb didn't go off and he soon had enough lead away from the trigger and the timing device that Chance and Charles could work to disarm the bomb, first they had to have the firemen spray water to cool off the bomb so they could work.

Finally, they got the bomb disarmed

Chance said, "I'm sure glad we didn't have to disarm the other bombs like this one."

Charles agreed and they watched a HazMat crew load the remains of the bomb into a special vehicle to take it to a safe place.

15

Hank matched another vehicle, which had crossed the border at White Rock, BC several days ago to his master list of recently purchased and licensed vehicles in Montreal.

The vehicle was a white Lincoln Stretch Limo carrying a Quebec License Plate.

Ron sent out the alert to state police in Washington, Oregon and California with the description and license number of the white Lincoln Stretch Limo.

Local police in Los Angeles and San Francisco were placed on high alert in the areas around the LA City Hall and the Golden Gate Bridge.

LA Police Department decided to block all exits off of Hollywood Freeway on the North, closed all traffic on 2nd Street, on the South, Figueroa on the West and Central and Alameda on the East preventing any vehicle from entering the area of City Hall.

When the driver of the white Lincoln tried to exit off of the Hollywood Freeway into the Civic Center, he was turned away, he tried going around to another street to get to the City Hall and was denied access.

Then a LA Police patrol car began following him and the chase was on. The driver of the limo sometimes was driving upward to a hundred miles an hour on regular city streets.

The patrol car was keeping close to him as the officers called for help from other officers and a police helicopter.

The limo managed to get on the San Diego Freeway and continued on it until reaching I-105 there he turned west toward Los Angeles International Airport.

The pilot of the police helicopter called ahead to have the exit at Sepulveda blocked, but only one police car had reached the exit before the limo arrived there.

The driver of the limo smashed into the patrol car hitting it on the left front quarter panel and spun the police car around as the limo continued toward the airport.

The helicopter pilot continued following the limo and watched as the car disappeared in the tunnel on Sepulveda and then hovered over the exit of the tunnel waiting for the limo to reappear, which didn't take long.

The limo turned into the Los Angeles International Airport and then into the limo waiting area, the helicopter pilot had a problem following the limo due to traffic landing at the airport.

He had to get out of the way of incoming aircraft. In the meantime the police officers who originally began the chase of the limo had arrived in the lot set aside for limos.

Arriving in the lot there must have been fifty white Lincoln Stretch Limos in the lot.

They got out of their car and they were soon joined by other police patrol cars.

Soon the entire lot was filled with LA Police, Airport Police and LA County Police Officers, they located the car they were looking for, but the driver was not in the car.

They didn't think the driver had time to get out of the lot before they arrived and the few drivers in the lot with their Limos didn't see anyone leave.

The officers begin searching through vehicles and one of them found the driver hiding underneath a limo a short distance from the car he had driven into the lot.

The officers contacted dispatch and advised them they had the limo and the driver, dispatch in turn notified the FBI and they notified the CIA, who had the team of scientist's enroute after disarming the bomb in Osoyoos, BC.

They were flying from Vancouver to Los Angeles. Tom received the message at eight-ten Eastern Time on the morning on September Eleven that the Los Angeles Police had found the limo.

At eight-fifteen, Tom got a message from Istanbul that they had finally made a deal with Zortman to get the time the bombs were set to go off, they were set for 9:11 AM Eastern Daily Time on 9-11.

They had less than an hour to disarm the bomb. The question was how far away from Los Angeles was the team of scientists coming from Vancouver.

They soon found out they were near Bakersfield.

Chance said, "We better get somebody with some welding equipment over to the limo and get the fuel tank opened up right now, so our people don't have to wait.

Anyway it going to be cutting it close to get the bomb disabled."

Tom contacted the FBI and advised them to make arrangements for a welder with a cutting torch to open up the auxiliary fuel tank before the scientists arrived.

The FBI had agents on the scene at Los Angeles International Airport and after they had a welder on site. They contacted Tom directly via cell phone. They asked what we should have the welder do to be ready for the team of nuclear scientist's enroute to their site.

Tom told them he would pass the phone over to Dr. Chance Taylor to guide the welder through the process of opening the auxiliary fuel tank to expose the bomb for the scientists.

Tom hand the phone to Chance, and Chance said, "Hello, is this the welder that going to help us with the problem of opening the fuel tank?"

"Yes, this is Joan Robinson. I'm your welder."

"Joan, is it Joan, is that right?"

"Yes, I'm Joan."

"Joan, I'm Chance Taylor and I'll explain what we need for you to do to help us. Joan, we've got a tough job here to get the auxiliary fuel tank opened up to exposed a nuclear bomb that's hidden in it and you need to follow my directions to be ready for the nuclear scientists that are coming to disarm this bomb, can you do it?"

"You tell me what I need to do, and I'll do it."

"Is there someplace you can take the car and get it up on a lift to get where you can work on the underside of the car?"

"No, there's no close place around here."

"OK, I know you've got some large forklifts around the airport, get two of them to come turn the car on its side."

"OK, I can do that."

Chance could hear Joan talking on her radio to a dispatcher and asking for two large forklifts to come to the limo parking lot in a hurry, it's an emergency.

The dispatcher told her, they're on the way.

Joan told Chance, the forklifts are on their way.

Chance said, "Joan, get down on the ground and look under the limo for a new looking fuel tank?"

"OK, I see it."

"Have the forklifts turn the car over so the fuel tank is close to the ground so you and the scientists can reach it to work on without standing on something."

"OK, I got it."

"When you get the tank were you can cut into it, the first thing you will need to do is be sure you empty any fuel in the tank and fill the tank with water, if you have a fire truck there with you they can fill it with a chemical to keep it from exploding while you're cut the other side of the tank.

You should see a seam that divides the tank between the part with fuel and the other part is where our suitcase bomb is, do you understand what I just told you?"

"Yeah, I got it and the forklifts are here and they are turning the car over now."

"Listen Joan, I don't want to rush you and have you make a mistake, but we need to do this as quickly as possible."

"OK, I got it, they turning the car over now. I won't have to drain the fuel out of the tank, because turning the car over just broke the nozzle to the fuel tank and the fuel is pour out.

"It's OK, because the fire department has just taken care of the spilled fuel and is filling the tank with some type of chemical, but I don't think it going to stay in the tank."

"Joan, try to put something on the tank to keep the chemical in the tank before you start cutting."

"OK, I got it to stop leaking; I put my bubble gum on the crack where the nozzle enters the tank."

"Good luck."

Chance could hear the noise of the cutting torch cutting the metal of the fuel tank.

At that moment Tom got a radio message, the plane carrying the nuclear scientists to Los Angeles had to make an emergency landing in Bakersfield.

The plane lost both of its engines and had to make a dead stick landing. The good news was everyone on the plane was all right.

Chance said, "What time is it?"

Tom replied, "It's eight-thirty."

"We've got a problem our team of scientists can't possible get to the bomb in time to disable it."

"What can we do, Chance?"

"I'm going to try to talk Joan through disabling the bomb, she our only hope right now. We don't have any of our people who could get there in time to help, we've only got until 9:11 our time to get the bomb disabled.

"I hope Joan can keep her cool as well as she has so far."

Joan said, "OK, I got the fuel tank cover cut off and I can see a thing that looks like a suitcase."

"Great work Joan, but I've got bad news. The scientists who were coming to defuse the bomb, well their plane just had to made an emergency landing in Bakersfield and there no way they can get there in time to disable the bomb.

"You're going to have to do it for me, can you do it?"

"God, I don't know, do I have a choice."

"No, you don't have a choice you've got to do it."

"OK, if I don't have a choice. I'll do it."

"Joan, not only does your life depend on doing this, but a lot of lives in Los Angeles will be depending on you doing it.

"We've got to start right now.

"We only have about twenty minutes to do this."

"OK, quit talking about it and tell me what to do."

"Good girl, here we go. First, take the suitcase out of the fuel tank and sit it on the ground and open up the snaps that hold the suitcase closed."

"OK, I'll do it."

"You should see metal tubing looking device that has an electronic controller attached to it by some wires, do you see it?"

"Do I see what?"

"Do you see the electronic device with a bunch of wires coming out of it?"

"OK, I see it."

"Good, you should be able to unscrew the electronic device from the metal cylinder, by turning it counter clock wise, do it."

"OK, I've got it unscrewed."

"Good lay it aside, now you should see a metal disc, it unscrews clockwise; unscrew it and put it carefully inside the suitcase, now look for a thing that looks like a small gun barrel, but it's sealed up on both ends."

"OK, I see it."

"Do the same thing to it, unscrew it by turning it counter clock wise."

"I can't get it to turn."

Chance asked Tom, "What time is it now?"

"Eight fifty-eight."

"Joan is there someone near you that can help you turn the barrel, if there is, get them to help you."

"I've got one of the FBI agents helping me, we've got it."

"Whew, good, now, there's an explosive charge in a round container in the bottom of the metal cylinder careful tip up the cylinder and it should fall out

"OK, it's out, what should I do with it?"

"Lay it in the suitcase, now you have one more electronic part that's in the bottom of the cylinder, it will probably take a Phillips Screwdriver to remove it. I think it's a left hand thread."

We don't have a Phillips Screwdriver. Yes, we do, one of the forklift drivers has one.

"OK, we got the screws out, what do I do now?"

"Just pull out the electronic controller the screws were holding in the cylinder."

"OK, I got it out."

"Congratulations Joan, you just disarmed a nuclear bomb."

"What was that clicking sound I just heard coming from the electronic controller that I took out of the cylinder."

"The sound is telling you its 9:11 AM in New York and that was the trigger to set off the nuclear bomb."

"Dr. Taylor, this is FBI Agent Tubby Smith, Joan fainted.

"Agent Smith, see if she all right."

"She OK, I caught her so she didn't fall on the pavement."

"Good, let me tell her she did a wonderful job."

"Joan, are you with me?"

"Sorry, I just blacked out for a moment, but I'm all right now."

"Thank you Joan you saved a lot of people's lives this morning.

Chance congratulated Charles and asked Tom to please thank all of the law enforcement agencies that helped find the bombs so they could be disarmed.

Tom said, "I'll get the word to Ron Parsons to let him know you wanted to have the agency thank all of the law enforcement officers who helped find the bombs for us so you could deactivate them."

Chance said to Charles, "Why are you so upset? Come on Charlie we got all of the bombs and America's safe."

Tom said, "I've just got word to bring both of you to CIA Headquarters in Langley. I guess they want to congratulate you for disarming the bombs and give you guys some metals or something."

16

When they flew into Washington DC, they landed at Andrews Air Force Base where a car was waiting for them, but instead of going to CIA Headquarters they were taken to a CIA training facility in Virginia.

Tom told them he didn't know what was going on for sure, but he guessed they wanted to debrief them before letting them go home.

The surprises just kept coming, because when they arrived they found the rest of their friends there. Then each of them were taken to individual rooms and locked up.

They were told the CIA still had a lot of questions they needed answers to, Charles and Annie tried to protest that they wanted to let their families know they were alive, but to no avail.

The CIA had some of their top interrogators on hand to ask the questions and they started with Chance.

The interrogators didn't introduce themselves, they just started firing question at a very tried and wiped out man.

"Chance, how come you decided to take your Corvette on the Moscow to Beijing Road Race?"

"I thought it would be an adventure and we would have a lot of fun."

"Did you, did you have fun?"

"Not exactly!"

"Why because the bombs didn't go off like you and your friends in al-Qaeda planned?"

"Are you out of your minds?"

"What do you know about this list we found hidden in Colonel Zmitrovitch pocket when he was captured?"

"What list, I've never seen any list, why don't you ask him?"

"He said we should ask you."

"Ask me what?"

"Ask you about the list you gave him?"

"I didn't give him or anybody any list."

"How did it feel to have to disarm all of those bombs you and Dr. Brown prepared for America?"

"Wonderful!"

"You mean you were happy about saving American lives."

"You damn right I was happy."

"Listen doctor if you're so innocent, why didn't you just let al-Qaeda kill you instead of making those bombs for them?"

"If it would have been just me, I would have. I just couldn't let my friends be killed if I didn't do what al-Sadr wanted me to do."

"You thought it was more important to save your friends then to save all of the people in America those bombs could have killed."

"Tell me what would you do?"

"Probably the same thing you did, and as it turned out you lost only one friend and stopped the bombs from exploding.

"Doctor Taylor you can go back to your room and take a shower and rest for awhile, OK?"

"OK, thanks."

Next, they brought Charles in and showed him a list of names that had been taken from Colonel Zmitrovitch with his name; Anmend and Kerida names on the list and they asked him why the colonel had a list with his name on it?

Almost before they started asking him the question, he started crying and told them. I helped them.

"Who did you help?"

"Anmend and Kerida, Anmend promised Kerida and I could go away and start a new live together with twenty-five million dollars in gold.

"I was so much in love with Kerida. I would have done anything to be with her and I was so tired of being in debt all of the time, my life with Cheryl was miserable.

"I had to get out. I hated my life and I hated my job."

"Why didn't you just get a divorce, if you wanted Kerida so bad?"

"I guess I couldn't stand admitting I had failed at anything, like my marriage.

"I just had to find a way out of all of my problems."

"Well doctor, you picked a hell of a way doing it."

"I know it. I can't believe all the things I put my best friend Chance through while he was trying to save all of us."

"Exactly, what did you do to help al-Qaeda?"

"I told Kerida about going on the road race with Chance and she told Anmend who must have told al-Qaeda, then Anmend told me if I helped them they would pay me twenty-five million dollars in gold and Kerida and I could live in Switzerland and never have to worry about anything the rest of our lives.

"I loved her so much and wanted to be with her.

"Then I talked Chance in to letting Kerida and Anmend go with us on the road race trip, then I encouraged Chance not to try to escape anymore and help me build the bombs."

"Did you know al-Qaeda was planning on killing all of your friends and the list we showed you were the people Colonel Zmitrovitch was instructed not to kill, you, Kerida and Anmend were the only names on the list."

"Some friend I am."

"Yeah!"

On the way back to his room Charles saw Colonel Zmitrovitch sitting and talking to Ron Parsons, laughing and having a drink.

The guard told Charles, Colonel Zmitrovitch, is one of our agents, who do you think made sure they didn't kill the Gypsies.

He supplied us with the information about the number of men al-Qaeda had at Mountain Top Lodge after al-Sadr left the Lodge, so Special Forces knew how many men they needed to rescue you and your friends.

"One day soon with a little help from us, we're sure he will escape and go back to Russia to help us track any more stolen nuclear material."

Next one in to be questioned was Kerida. She only told them she loved Charles and would do anything to be with him and to help her brother returns to Indonesia, as its ruler.

"Al-Qaeda promised to help him take control of Indonesia and let him rule it as his grandfather had."

When Anmend was questioned he admitted nothing except he planned to return to Indonesia and rule it one day very soon.

The CIA doubt he would ever return to Indonesia. He would be a guest of the United States for the rest of his life.

Annie was still fuming about not being able to call her parents and let them know she was alive. When they brought her into be questioned, a CIA agent handed her a phone and told her to call them.

She did and felt so much better after talking to her parents. Her dad said he told her mother, he never believed she had drown, she told her Dad you're never going to believe what really happened to me.

After I get home I'll tell you all about it.

He certainly wouldn't believe it.

The CIA told Curtis they were sorry to hold him for so long and about losing his friend PJ.

Curtis told them he understood and one day soon they would be able to take their families to see a movie about what happened to them.

Shannon O'Hara was thanked for her co-operation and help. She was told the America Government appreciated her help and for her understanding of being held for so long after she had been freed from al-Qaeda.

She said, "I understand and I'm glad I could be of some help to you."

Then they told her she would be paid for her time and her help. They gave her a check for one hundred thousand dollars.

They told Shannon they made arrangements to fly her home to London and had a plane waiting for her at Andrews Air Force Base.

She asked to see Chance Taylor, but was told no, she couldn't see him right now.

They still had more questions for him to answer to help them finish their report to CIA Headquarters.

She tried one more time by asking them if she could talk to Tom Parker, because she thought if she could talk with Tom, he would help her get to see Chance.

The answer was no. Tom Parker was no longer here, he had been called to CIA Headquarters for debriefing about his mission.

She wasn't going to get the opportunity to talk with Chance, she needed to see him before she was whisked away by the CIA.

She thought about trying crying lots of tears, but decided these guys wouldn't give their own mother a break.

So she asked if she could leave Chance a note.

They said, sorry you don't have time your car is waiting and they're holding a plane for you, you have to go right now.

What choice did she have, but to go?

The agents she had been talking with walked her out of the interrogation room and led her directly to a waiting car to take her to Andrews.

She didn't like it, she wanted to see and talked to Chance, because she hadn't had a chance to see or talk with him since their one night together at Mountain Top Lodge.

She didn't know if he thought she went to bed with every guy she saw or if he felt about her the way she felt about him.

She knew she was in love with him and she wasn't going to get the chance to tell him so.

The CIA was making arrangements to have the three prisoners Charles, Kerida and Anmend moved to a federal prison to await trial.

When the federal marshals went into Charles' room to transfer him to a federal prison, they found he had killed himself by hanging himself with the cords from the draperies. He tied the cords around a ceiling fan.

While they were putting him on a stretcher to load him in a hearse. Chance came into the room, got down on his knees next to the stretcher and held him and softly cried and asked, "Why did you do it, why Charlie?"

After the hearse took Charles' body away, he asked about Shannon, where was she?

It took a few minutes before anyone would give him an answer, but finally one of the agents told him she left to go home to London.

Chance couldn't believe she left without at least telling him good bye.

Two weeks later after Chance was back home in Albuquerque he heard his doorbell ring and when he opened the door he saw Annie and two men he didn't know standing there.

Annie said, "Dr. Chance Taylor, I want you to meet Jack Clayton, Vice President of Sales for Chevrolet and Sammy Bradshaw with our advertising firm.

"We're here to give you something for helping America in its time of a real crisis."

Outside Chance could see several people including, Curtis La Salle, who was directing a cameraman who was filming everything going on.

Chance shook hands with Mr. Clayton and Mr. Bradshaw.

Jack Clayton said, "Dr. Taylor would you please come outside with us?"

Chance followed Mr. Clayton outside and when they got out to where they could see Chance's driveway.

He saw a big lump in his driveway covered up with a fancy canvass cover.

Mr. Clayton said, "Dr. Taylor on behalf of the Chevrolet Division of General Motors. We would like to present this small token of our appreciation for the courage and duty you preformed for your country and your fellow Americans."

As Mr. Clayton finished his statement, the canvass was removed from a brand new bright yellow Corvette.

Mr. Clayton handed Chance two sets of keys for the car.

"Mr. Clayton, I don't know what to say, except thank you and thanks Chevrolet."

Chance went over to look at his new car and Annie told him. Do you remember all of the plastic wrap I put on your "58" Vet, you know the stuff you complained about.

Well, it saved your car from the ocean and the CIA is bringing it back to you in the next few weeks, as soon as I finish going over it to be sure it's in perfect condition again.

Chance pulled her close to him and kissed her and said, "Thank you Annie Taylor!"

Then Chance said, "I've quit my job and enrolled in Harvard Medical School and plan to do medical research in the future, but before I start medical school. I'm going to London to ask Shannon O'Hara to marry me.

"It seems when my Gypsy friend, Juanita told my fortune she was right about everything.

"Since, I didn't get to talk to Shannon before she left to go home to London. It took me a few weeks to decide if I want to contact her.

"I thought when she left so abruptly. I thought she didn't want to see me again.

"I finally called her on the telephone and she told me she begged to speak to me, but the CIA wouldn't let her. Instead they whisked her away and put her on a plane back to London.

"Then I realized I was in love with her and couldn't live without her.

"So, I'm on the flight she's working tomorrow night from Chicago to London. She doesn't know I'm on it, because I wanted to surprise her.

"See I never told her I when I was coming to see her, just that I was coming before I started to Harvard and she certainly doesn't know why I'm coming."

17

hance put his new Corvette in the garage and thought it was a wonderful gift the people at Chevy gave him. He had his bags packed for his trip to London and was getting ready to call a taxi when his telephone rang.

He picked up the phone and answered it, "Chance Taylor."

A voice on the telephone said, "Chance, this is Shannon O'Hara do you have time to talk?"

"Sure Shannon. I have some time to talk, however I was getting ready to go on a trip."

"Well are you sure you have time to talk to me?"

"Shannon is there someplace. I could call you back in about an hour?"

"Chance, I'm so sorry I bother you. I should have called you sooner to be sure you were home."

"Where are you?"

"I'm in Albuquerque, New Mexico. I decided to come take a look at this place you live so I took some time off. I'm so sorry you not going to be here to show me around."

"Where are you Shannon?"

"I'm at the airport, maybe I could see you if you're flying out on your trip,"

"That sounds good Shannon. I'll be at the airport in about thirty minutes and we can visit for a little while before I go on my trip."

Chance flew out the door and backed his new Corvette out of the garage and raced to the airport as quickly as possible.

As he was driving to see Shannon he thought he wasn't the only one who could come up with surprises. What a surprise Shannon pulled on him!

Arriving at the airport he parked his car in the short term parking area and raced into the terminal looking for Shannon.

He couldn't decide how he should act when he saw her, should he play it cool. Maybe he should give her a kiss on the cheek or what? He didn't know how he should greet her.

As he made his way through the entrance and started looking for her in the front of the terminal he suddenly saw her.

She was as beautiful as he remembered, maybe more beautiful.

She saw Chance at the same time and began walking toward him, then she began running to him and he to her.

He grabbed her up in his arms and kissed her hard on her lips and he knew all the people in the terminal must be looking at them.

He also felt every man in the terminal would have liked to change places with him.

As he sat her back down on her feet, he said, "Shannon, I love you so much I was on my way to London to ask you to marry me.

Shannon replied, "Yes, I'll marry you and I've saved you a trip."

"We've got so much we need to talk about, let's go to my house and talk."

"That's a wonderful idea."

She stepped back away from him and he really looked her over.

She was dressed in a great looking yellow skirt with a white blouse with yellow daisies embroidered on it that matched the color of her skirt. Her hair was longer than the last time he saw her and it was beautiful done.

He couldn't wait to hold her away from prying eyes.

He took her hand and started out to his car when he realized he hadn't asked her if she had a bag somewhere.

She did have a bag, but she left it where she was standing waiting for him to come to see her. They went back to get her bag where she left it and at the same time a security guard was looking the bag over very carefully and was about to pick it up and have it destroyed.

Shannon said, "I'm so sorry officer. I left my bag here when I went to meet my boyfriend. I'm so sorry."

Then she flashed a killer smile in his direction.

He said, "Lady, do you know what kind of trouble you could have caused us leaving a bag here unattended, it could have been filled with explosives or a nuclear bomb for all we knew."

Shannon again told him how sorry she was and flashed that smile at him again and with a great Irish brogue, she said,

"Oh officer, I am truly so sorry to cause you problems and I promise it will never happen again."

The security guard had no choice except to say, "All right young lady, but please look out for your things when you're in an airport from now on."

In the same brogue she replied, "I surely will officer."

All Chance could do was stand back and listen and smile to himself about how Shannon handled herself.

Chance picked up her bag.

This time they made it to his car.

Shannon said, "Is this the same car you were going to race?"

"No, it's a new Corvette, the Chevrolet Company gave it to me for help stop the attack on America, isn't wonderful?"

"I love it, it's so pretty."

Chance drove to his home as quickly as he could. He couldn't wait to get Shannon alone with him.

As soon as they got inside the house he pulled her close to him and kissed her over and over and between kisses. He asked her again to marry him?"

Shannon answered, "Yes, yes I will marry you."

The next thing he asked her was if she would like to see his house and the response was, yes, maybe your bedroom.

They went directly to his bedroom and he pulled her close to him and began kissing her and running his hand up under her skirt and she said, "Why don't we get undressed and go to bed."

"You have wonderful ideas Shannon."

He began taking off his clothes as she was busy taking hers off.

Chance was faster than she was, he had his clothes off and watching her take hers off and when she was down to her yellow panties that matched her outfit.

He told her he would be happy to help her.

He reached for the waistband of those pretty yellow panties and slowly began pulling them down as if he was opening a precious gift and she stood very still and enjoyed every moment that he took taking them off.

She had been looking at him remembering the first time she saw him laying naked beside the small stream in Romania and admiring his body and talking to him in English, when she thought he couldn't understand what she was saying.

He still looked as good to her now as when she first saw him and he was about to make love to her.

She took him by his hand and led him to the bed and lay down in front of him so he could get a good look at all of her body.

That was almost too much for Chance. He stood there looking at her and making love with her in his mind already.

He carefully slipped into bed with her afraid he might be dreaming, but he wasn't dreaming she was really there in his bed.

They made love for the rest of the day and when it was dark he said, "We have to have something to eat and drink."

Shannon agreed.

They got out of bed, dressed and drove to the nearest café they could find. They discovered they were almost famished and both ordered two dinners.

Chance ate both of his meals and then finished what was left on the plate of Shannon's second dinner.

Chance said quietly, "Shannon, I never knew making love caused one to be so hungry."

"Neither did I, but it was wonderful!"

They decided right then to get married in Las Vegas.

Chance make arrangement for them to fly to Vegas tonight, he didn't want to give her too much time to think about getting married and taking a chance that Shannon would changing her mind.

While they were waiting for their flight to Las Vegas, Chance took a diamond engagement ring from his pocket and placed it on her finger.

It fit, which surprised both of them and he did have wedding bands for both of them as well.

Shannon couldn't believe Chance had planned to come to London to ask her to marry him and had even bought rings for them for their wedding.

They flew to Vegas, got their marriage license and were married at "The Little Chapel of The Flowers" before the night was over.

They had a wonderful wedding ceremony and they were both glad they decide to come to Vegas and get married and not have a big church wedding.

They checked in at Caesars' Palace and found the honeymoon suite was open so they took it.

It was a beautiful suite, suitable for an Irish Princess and Shannon loved it. Shannon was Chance's Irish Princess and he knew they would have many happy loving years together.

18

Tom Parker was having a long conversation with Ron Parsons, Deputy Director of the CIA about the case that Tom had been in charge of with, its highly successful conclusion.

Ron told him what a great job he did and said, "I'm sure you're getting another Presidential Award for your service, even if the general public will never know what you and your team did to protect America.

"Tom, I don't know what I would do without you, you're the luckiest agent in the CIA."

"Ron I don't think you will have to worry. I'm sure I will never retire until I can't walk anymore or one of the bad guys get's me, or you send Hank to help me again.

"I have to say he did a great job, but he drives me crazy doing it!"

"Tom for once I'm giving you a job which doesn't have much risk to it. I want you to accompany Annie Taylor, she with Chevy, you do remember her don't you?"

"Of course I remember her. Ron, I always remember beautiful women."

"OK, you remember her, she finished going over Dr. Chance Taylor's "58" Corvette and it's ready to be delivered to him at his home in Albuquerque, New Mexico.

"I want you to go with her to represent the CIA."

"Well Ron, it sounds like a tough job, but I guess somebody has to do it, right."

"Call Annie and make arrangements to meet her in Albuquerque to be there when Dr. Taylor's car is returned to him.

"Just one more thing before you leave, after you finish that assignment come back to the office and I'll give you your new mission.

"I'm not sending you back to Istanbul. I need you around here and from now on, you report directly to me."

Tom called Annie at her office in Michigan and made arrangements to meet her next week in Albuquerque to return Chance's Corvette to him.

They both agreed it should be lots of fun to see Chance's reaction of seeing his car after it was lost in the Black Sea.

Annie told Tom, Chance's "58" Corvette looks like it came directly from the factory and it should look like that, since the car was totally rebuilt in the Chevrolet Factory.

The following week, Tom and Annie meet at the Albuquerque Airport.

Tom was surprised to see Chevrolet had sent Curtis La Salle to film the event, but it was good to see him again.

They picked up two rental cars and proceed to follow the truck carrying the Corvette to Chance's house.

Tom didn't know Curtis La Salle and a cameraman would be there to film delivering the car back to Chance, but thought it would be a nice thing to do.

Curtis told him I have to complete the film and returning the Corvette back to the same driveway it left from it will bring the story to a close.

Annie said, "I called Chance to make sure he would be home today for a special delivery and he said he promised to be home to receive his special delivery."

When they parked in front of Chance's house the truck carrying the Corvette back into the driveway to unload the Corvette.

The driver and his helper put down ramps to back the car off of the truck and the car was soon on Chance's driveway.

All of these actives were being filmed by Curtis' cameraman and now all they had to do was ring the doorbell and have Chance be reunited with his Corvette.

The cameraman was all sit up to film the event and Tom and Annie, were on the porch ready to ring the doorbell.

Curtis said, "OK Annie, ring the bell."

Annie rang the bell and the front door of Chance's house slowly opened and the waiting parties outside that door were in for a real surprise, because it wasn't Chance Taylor, who opened the door it was Shannon O'Hara!"

Annie didn't know what to say and Tom just stood there wondering what was going on?

Shannon said, "Chance will be right here, he's in the bathroom."

Tom recovered and responded, "Ms. O'Hara it's wonderful to see you again, but we weren't expecting you to open Chance's door!"

"I'm sorry if you're disappointed that it wasn't Chance who opened the door and it's not Ms. O'Hara anymore, it's Mrs. Taylor, Mrs. Chance Taylor!"

"Congratulations Shannon." Tom said.

Annie joined in "Its wonderful Shannon, Chance is a lucky man."

Chance arrived at the door in time for him to hear that he was a lucky man, he thought he certainly was.

The whole scene had been captured on film and the script couldn't have been written any better in Hollywood.

Curtis was thrilled with the scene for his film, because nothing lights up a film like two beautiful women and these two women were.

Tom regained his purpose of being here and said, "Chance, on behalf of the CIA and the Chevrolet Division of General Motors, Annie Taylor and I wants to present you with your completely refurbished 1958 Corvette, it's now at home from the Black Sea."

Annie handed Chance two sets of new keys for his Corvette.

Chance in turned gave one set of keys to Shannon and he said, "Darling, this is your wedding present, since I haven't had time to buy you one yet."

Hand in hand, Chance and Shannon ran down the driveway to see how the Corvette looked.

Chance shouted, "It looks like it just came off of a showroom floor."

Annie said, "Well it never made it on a showroom floor, but it comes directly from the factory to you."

Shannon exclaimed, "Oh Chance, I love my wedding present, thank you and thank everyone for getting the car back and fixing it up.

"I know Chance loved this car, so it means even more to me, that he would give it to me."

Shannon and Chance shared a kiss and Curtis shouted, "Cut, my film is finished.

Annie said, "Chance, since I got back to Chevy I got a new job, they made me the chief engineer on the Corvette. If I hadn't got the assignment going with you on the road race. I would never have gotten the job.

"Thanks, Chance for giving me the opportunity of going on the trip with you and your car."

Chance replied, "That's wonderful and you did a wonderful job of looking after my car, if after it went down in the Black Sea."

Chance, gave Annie and hug a kiss and thanked her once more for the great job she did.

Tom never enjoyed an assignment as much as this one, as he was thinking about it when he walked into CIA Headquarters the following Monday morning, wondering what kind of assignment he would draw next.

He soon found out, Ron told him he was to concentrate on finding clues to the whereabouts of Dr. al Sadr and when he found out where al-Sadr was.

Tom was to captured or kill al-Sadr. Ron didn't care much about which one he did. Just get that son-of-a-bitch!

Today, Hank was reading through stack and stack of newspapers and magazines that had acclimated in his absents and in his personnel file he now had two new pieces of paper the likes he never had in his file before, since he been employed by the CIA.

Hank had two commendations, one from the Director of the CIA and one from the President of the United States, which were placed on top of all of those copies of verbal warnings for unauthorized trips.

Hank found an article in a Miami newspaper about several boats being picked up by the Coast Guards near Key West, loaded with Cuban men and he remembered a article about a speech Castro made years ago about the Florida Keys actually belonging to Cuba and being stolen by America.

Hank took the two articles and ran as fast as he could into Ron Parsons' office and said, "Ron, Castro is sending landing parties to take over the Florida Keys, you know a long time ago he said we stolen the keys from Cuba years ago."

Ron screamed, "Oh, god, help us, here we go again!"